PERSIAN FABLES AND FAIRY TALES

Keyvan Moghissi

PAPER AGE
PUBLISHING

PERSIAN FABLES AND FAIRY TALES

First Published by Paper Age Publishing 2020

paperagepublishing@gmail.com

ISBN 978-1-9996143-9-3

Typesetting by bookindle.uk

For my Mother

FOREWORD

In 1935 the country known for centuries as *Persia* became *Iran.* Since then, particularly in 1955, it has been suggested that *Persia* and *Iran* should be interchangeable names. The debate is continuing as to whether, for historical reasons, the name Iran should be employed.

This is a collection of old tales which are documented or passed on from ancient times, from one generation to the next; the change of the name – Persia or Iran – has had no influence on the legends and mythology which form their basic character or substance. Here, I present an overview of the stories to which I, as a child and adolescent, have been exposed, either through the family (notably my grandmother), or school.

The legends, mythology and fictional characters are timeless – originated by Persian writers, raconteurs and ordinary people. They have been used by many authors before but the narratives I present are a way of introducing these Persian tales using my personal imagination and improvisation; a method which typically is used by a solo musical instrument, players such as a violinist, in Persian classical music.

The main audience I had in mind when I was planting the seeds of the project was, typically, the generation of descendants of Persians/Iranians who may be keen to know more about their culture, folklore or legends and the mythology of their ancestors. Typical examples are my own son and grandsons.

I also hope that others interested in the legends and mythology of the Persians, which in all aspects rival the

Greeks, might be interested to read and discover a flavour of what is the culture of the Persians.

I have a great pleasure in acknowledging with gratitude the efforts of my friend Kate Dixon who for many years has partnered my scientific and clinical writings. She has used her expertise in English language to read and edit the manuscript of this, the Persian Fables and Fairy Tales.

"Mico", Michael Alexander Moghissi has devoted many hours to follow through the publication of "granddad's work". He certainly has been an inspiring young man for me, and I am grateful for his support and devotion.

Sirpa Pajunen-Moghissi has designed the cover of the book, and Heather Burton has done the hand drawn illustrations, my heartful thanks goes to both. I thank Janet Melvin for formatting and preparing the manuscript for publication.

Finally, Alex, my wife has been an encouraging source.

CONTENTS

INTRODUCTION

I believe no Persian story book can ignore Persian legends and mythology and no Persian legends or mythology could be narrated without mentioning the Avesta – the Zoroastrian holy book – or Ferdowsi's Shahnameh: The Book of Kings and Rumi's Masnavi, a colossal six volume mystical poetry.

Zoroastrianism

This is one of the world's oldest, if not the oldest, religion. It promotes the belief of the oneness of God: Monotheism.

It was founded by the Prophet Zoroaster[1] or Zarathustra in ancient Persia approximately 3500 years ago.

Other ancient contemporary civilizations, such as the Greeks, Chinese or Egyptians, were either idolatries, or believed in many Gods: Polytheism.

The symbol of Zoroastrianism or Zoroaster taken from the ruins of Persepolis is shown below.

Zoroastrians use the Avesta as their sacred text. The Avesta contains hymns, rituals and spells against demons.

Symbol of Zoroastrianism

[1] Zoroaster (Zarathustra)
"Zoroastrianism" *Encyclopædia Iranica*, online edition, 2015, available at: http://www.iranicaonline.org/articles/zoroastrianism

Ferdowsi (Abu ʾl-Qasim Ferdowsi)

In terms of volume of work, content and historical importance, Ferdowsi is the most impressive Persian poet, who lived in the 10th century (AD 940-1020). He is the author of Shahnameh[2] – the Book of Kings – which is the world's longest epic poetry book by a single author.

A lot of Persian history of the kings and most of the Persian mythology is based on Shahnameh. The original 10th century manuscript no longer exists. There is a 13th century manuscript in the Biblioteca Nazionale Centrale di Firenze (Central National Library of Florence). There is also a manuscript in the London National Library.

Ferdowsi was born into a family of landowners (*Dehqans*) in AD 940 in the village of Paj, near the city of Tus, in the Khorasan Province of north-eastern Persia.

Little is known about Ferdowsi's early life and education. He began work on the *Shahnameh (The Book of Kings)* which is the greatest of his writings around AD 977.

Shahnameh took a good 30 years to be completed in March 1010 and it was the promise of a generous reward (One Gold Piece for every couplet) by Ghaznavid, Sultan Mahmud which was an incentive to spend hours and hours to write it. The poet agreed to receive the money as a lump sum when he had completed the work. He planned to use it to rebuild the dykes in his native Tus.

On completion the sultan apparently prepared the 60,000 gold pieces, one for every couplet, as it had been agreed and issued an order to deliver it to the author.

---

2 Shahnameh: https://en.wikipedia.org/wiki/Shahnameh

However, this did not materialise and instead a caravan of camels loaded with silver pieces was sent to the poet. It is a matter of debate, conjecture and speculation as to whether Sultan Mahmud had a change of mind or his Vizirs and officials cheated Ferdowsi.

The legend has it that Ferdowsi was in a public bath house when he received the silver pieces. He was hurt and greatly offended and decided to give away the entirety of the money to the Bath Keepers, the Slaves who carried the money and whoever happened to be around.

This in turn was an insult to the Sultan who did not know all the facts at the time.

Ferdowsi fled to Khorasan, having first written a satire on Mahmud, and spent most of the remainder of his life in exile. Mahmud eventually learned the truth about the courtier's deception and had him punished. He also ordered the 60,000 pieces of gold to be sent again to Ferdowsi. By this time (AD 1020) the aged Ferdowsi had returned to Tus, but never saw his gold. It is documented that, as the caravan bearing the money entered the gates of Tus, a funeral procession exited the gates on the opposite side: the poet had died from a heart attack in AD 1020.

I remember reading this legend in Farsi when I was about 10 years old and was terribly upset and distressed and asked my grandmother if this was true. She said it was not the Sultan who had changed his mind but his right hand Vizir – who was dishonest and had originally changed gold pieces replacing them with silver and that he was punished for it.

Ferdowsi was buried in his own garden, because he was

denied burial in the cemetery of Tus by local clerics. Later, however, a Ghaznavids governor of Khorasan constructed a mausoleum over the grave. The tomb, was rebuilt between 1928 and 1934 by the Society for the National Heritage of Iran on the orders of Rezā Shāh Pahlavi.

Statue of Ferdowsi

Rumi and Masnavi

Rumi was a 13th century Persian mystic poet who is an important figure in Sufism of the Sunni sect of Islam. His full name is Jalal al-Din Muhammad Rumi[3] (known as Mawlana, meaning our Master, or Mawlawī meaning my master). More simply and popularly he is known as *Rumi.*

---

3 *RUMI, JALĀL AL-DIN," Encyclopædia Iranica,* online edition, 2014, available at: http://www.iranicaonline.org

He was born in Balkh (in 1207) which in present day is in Afghanistan but at the time, it was part of the post Islamic greater Persia.

Rumi has a unique place in Islam in Asia because of his writing, notably Masnavi which is considered by many as the Persian Quran. It is a massive book of six volumes and 27000 verses. Rumi wrote principally in Farsi, Arabic, Turkish and occasionally in Greek. This makes him a multi-national poet (without frontiers) in many of the Asian, Islamic countries.

He died at the age of 66 (in 1273) in Konya in Turkey where there is a monument and a museum of Rumi.

Although Masnavi has been translated into many languages, the manuscript is in Farsi and still easily understood by the modern Farsi speaking nations.

Poems in Masnavi have been a source of inspiration for many of the Iranian composers and musicians who have used the text and verses for vocal music.

Statue of Rumi in Buca (Izmir, Turkey)

Simurgh

The word Simurgh in Farsi, the Persian/Iranian language, is made up of 'Si' meaning thirty and Murgh, meaning a female bird, a hen. In the case of Simurgh, the female bird has been recorded to be a large eagle, as big as 30 birds.

Although Simurgh is a legendary bird in Persian mythology, many of the eastern countries acknowledge this bird as one of their country's legends. Throughout Persian influenced territories: Iraq, Arabia, part of India, Afghanistan and the countries bordering the Caspian sea, such as Georgia, medieval Armenia and the Byzantine Empire, the Simurgh is portrayed as a peacock with the head of a dog and the claws of a lion. She is agile, powerful, an invincible creature of benevolence. It could catch and lift into the air large animals and transport them long distances with the speed of light.

The Simurgh always stood on the side of the oppressed, injured and slaves. She would fight evil and always win. If you have the Simurgh as a friend, as a person who is good, injured or in need, she will give you a bunch of her feathers; this will bring her to your aid.

In some legends you will burn a feather to get the Simurgh's help, in others you only needed to throw a feather into the air and, in no time, Simurgh will be at your service; to advise, assist or do whatever it takes to help.

The power of healing of Simurgh had been documented for centuries and her symbol has become the emblem for Medicine in Persia and Iran, instead of the Staff or Rod of Asclepius which is employed in many of the countries in the world.

Sirmurgh lived on the highest peak of the Alborz Mountain chain, Damavand, and nested in a legendary tree – Gaokerena – known in Zoroastrian legends as the mighty and mythical Haoma plant that had healing properties when eaten. The juice from its fruit gave the elixir of immortality. The name *Gaokerena* means 'ox horn' or 'cow ear'.

How old is Simurgh? The simple answer is that this creature is ageless. She is mentioned in the Avesta, the Zoroastrian book circa 6th century BC.

In post Islamic Persia, the most famous appearance of Simurgh is in Ferdowsi's epic *Shahnameh* – the Book of Kings (between 977 and 1010 CE).

Figure above: Simurgh, the Symbol of Healing and Medicine in Iran

Figure below: Left: Caduceus Right: The Rod of Asclepius:

Image above: Simurgh Bas-Relief in Persepolis

Image below: Simurgh image in Shahnameh

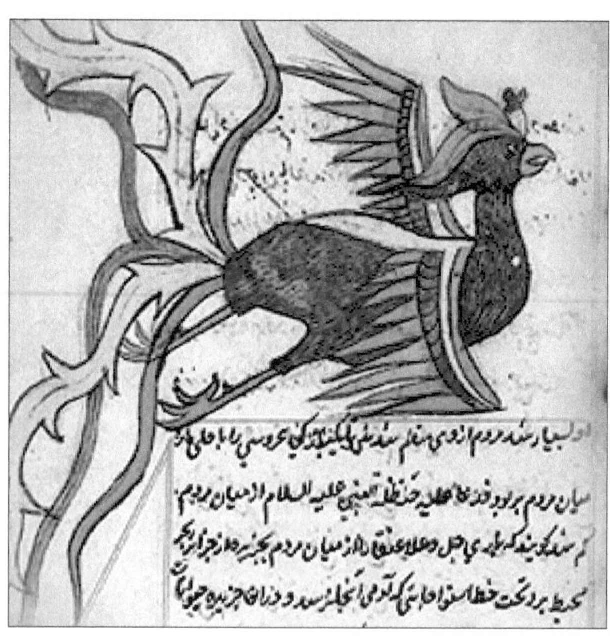

An Introduction to Mullah Nasr al-Din (the Mullah)

The word Mullah means a Muslim, educated in Islamic theology and laws. In large parts of the Muslim world, it also is the name given to local Islamic clerics or mosque leaders.

Mullah Nasr al-Din is a legend in the Asian and Islamic world. He is identified as being a simple man or a kind of fool on the surface, but he is clever, with a complicated character deep down. He is, essentially a kind man and an eccentric, but at times unpredictable giving the impression of being a joker in order to address a social issue.

For those who are born into and have knowledge of the Persian culture, there is no difficulty in appreciating the Mullah's place and in recognizing his anecdotes as being like a joke but with a more profound implied meaning and to appreciate the moral of his adventures.

Many countries consider Mullah as one of their own. The Persian substantiate their claim by the fact, they believe, that he was born in the city of Khoy in West Azerbaijan, in Persia, and was educated in Khorasan in the north-west of Persia/Iran.

There are many versions of any given anecdote of Mullah Nasr al-Din. However, basically, the gist of the stories are the same; variations depend on the raconteur or writer.

This accounts for the variations in many of the stories; it is up to the storyteller to tell a story using the gist of the original story.

This phenomenon of improvisation in interpretation is a characteristic of Persian music as well.

In this context my Mullah's stories are unique to me but based on the originals I have encountered as a child or a teenager.

Some characteristics of Mullah Nasr al-Din are acknowledged universally:

Mullah is definitely an unusual being.

He has a very close understanding and relationship with his donkey.

He rides his donkey backwards as the donkey knows all the roads and it is too stressful for Mullah to watch the upcoming road and events. He would rather enjoy the view in a more relaxed way.

Mullah is not only a religious leader in his community, but he is a judge, a wizard and a counsellor.

Now-Ruz

The term Now-Ruz in Farsi is comprised of Now – meaning new, and Ruz – meaning day: literally "New Day", or "*Equinox*".

Its origin is Zoroastrian-Persian and it has been celebrated for over 3000 years in Persia, Iran and many other countries.

Traditionally the Now-Ruz is a festival of life and a celebration of the revival of nature after the long dark winter nights.

The basic concept and tradition of Now-Ruz has not changed for centuries. Festivities stretch over 4 phases of events, starting 2-3 weeks before the actual day:

1. **Khaneh-Takani** which literally means shaking/airing the home. This starts two to three weeks before the Now-Ruz, when people start spring cleaning, washing curtains and Persian carpets and getting rid of unwanted clothing.

2. **Chaharshanbeh Suri** – chaharshanbeh, means Wednesday and Suri means fire or redness - is a ritual of making a bonfire and jumping over it, singing and dancing on the last Wednesday evening before the Now-Ruz.

3. **Now-Ruz** – this is really a festival for everyone, especially the children, who traditionally, were provided with new items of clothing; they would receive presents from parents and immediate family such a grandmother, aunts and uncles. In Tehran no child would even think of giving presents to the parents or grownups, not even to brothers or sisters.

On the morning of the Now-Ruz it was the tradition that the children, of any age, visited parents and grandparents. The

Scheme of
NOW-RUZ
The Persian New Year
BEGINNING OF MARCH
KHANEH-TAKANI
SPRING CLEANING OF HOUSE & CARPETS
WEDNESDAY FESTIVAL - LAST WEDNESDAY BEFORE NOW-RUZ FESTIVAL
CHAHAR-SHANBEH-SURI
JUMPING OVER BONFIRE OF SPRING CLEANING STUFF
3-7 DAYS
21st MARCH
NOW-RUZ
NEW CLOTHES, VISIT FAMILY & EXCHANGE PRESENTS
13 DAYS AFTER NOW-RUZ
SEEZDEH-BEDAR
FAMILY & COMMUNITY PICNIC

oldest person in the family, such as the grandfather, would never go and visit children first. Tradition demanded that the grandfather's door was open for children and grandchildren to visit and wish him a happy Now-Ruz on the very first day of the Now-Ruz period which extended up to a week.

Grandfather usually had a bag full of coins (depending on his financial situation anything from small gold coins to copper ones) to give as a present to the children and grandchildren.

During the next few days of the new year, family and friends visited one another, but there was an unwritten rule that it was the role of the youngers to visit the elders first.

Incidentally, one essential ingredient of the Now-Ruz has always been to have a table on which is displayed what is called Haft Seen or Haft Sin (Haft means 7 and Sin is the letter of Farsi language alphabet equivalent of S in English). So, on the table is displayed at least seven items whose names start with Sin/S, such as:

Sabzsh (green wheat, barley or lentil sprouts grown in a dish)
Sonbol (Hyacine)
Seeb (Apple)
Samanoo (Persian delicacies)
Seer (Garlick)
Somaq (Sumac)
Serkeh (vinegar)

4. Seezdeh-Bedar – comprises of Seezdah, meaning, thirteen and Bedar signifying outdoors or outing.

Thirteen days after the first day of Now-Ruz – 2nd April – is the official end of the New Year festivities and it is marked by a day of outings and picnics.

In the 1930s and 1940s, outside the cities were fields where rich or poor would spend a day in nature.

In Tehran these fields were bright, with Narcissi in flower and many blooming trees.

In recent years parks and public places are the venue for Seezdeh-Bedar.

Rumour has it that the strict Islamic Republic of Iran and its overpowering clergy tried hard to abolish the un-Islamic Now-Ruz and the pagan festivities of Chahrshanbeh-Suri and Seezdeh-Bedar, without any success. When it comes to Now-Ruz and the issue of Islam, most Iranians are first Persian or Iranian, and then Moslem, which is not a 'native' Iranian religion.

Ali's Donkey and Mullah Nasr al-Din

One of the civic duties of Mullah Nasr al-Din (the Mullah) was to engage with people and provide counsel to his parishioners.

Once a week on the Thursday he would give audience in his town and deliver his advice to whoever was in need of resolution to a problem. In effect this was the Mullah's Citizen's Advice Bureau, which was appreciated by the people who sometimes came from far afield to consult Mullah, the wise man. Mullah enjoyed the event.

The service he was providing was free of charge but if someone wanted to give him a "present" he would appreciate and allow them to invite him for a glass of tea or preferably lunch after Friday morning prayers.

Most of these audiences were in public within a room provided by the Town Council (Shahr-dari). Occasionally people wanted a more private audience. This was also possible and yet again, free of charge, but a sack of rice or shoulder of lamb would be gratefully received and would be rewarded by a blessing from God delivered by the Mullah.

Ali was a street trader with a donkey called "Zerang" which had served him well for a good 15 years, but it was now getting a bit too old for carrying a load for a whole day. Zerang was also slightly lame and was rather irritable, braying too many times and he was not quite predictable in the lower intestinal tract department!!

Ali knew the Mullah well and regularly went to the Mosque where Mullah was the principal preacher. He decided to consult Mullah and seek advice about what he needed to do with Zerang. Therefore, he asked for a private audience with Mullah.

The meeting was friendly and during the consultation he left Zerang with Mullah's donkey, sharing a delicious meal of grass hay and barley straw with a drink of cool, clean water.

"Well, Ali Khan, "how can I help?" asked the Mullah.

"Jenab[4] eh Mullah, right now I have a very tight schedule of a delivery of water melons within the district of Shahpoor Street and I am losing money because I can't pick up my load on time from Darvazeh Qazvin (the gate of Qazvin) on time. Also, I am not able to deliver watermelons to all my customers during the day. By the time I reach my last customer, it is near midnight and I have to pick up my next day's load at 5 o'clock in the morning."

Mullah could not quite see what the problem was as Ali, true to the oriental fashion of conversation, was not spelling out the problem.

Ali was going round and round saying what he could not do but still not getting to the point, until Mullah said "What does your donkey Zerang think?"

"Well" said Ali; "The problem is actually Zerang."

"So, tell me," coaxed Mullah.

My donkey has a number of problems; it is slow and cannot run without stopping or sitting. He has become noticeably lame; he is difficult with his meals and unfortunately cannot control his bladder and bowels.

---

4 Jenab means 'Excellency'

“Alright”, said Mullah who at last understood the problem. In essence Ali’s donkey was old, lame, could not control his bladder or bowels and was becoming useless for work.

“My friend, what you want to do is to find a good home for your donkey that still has some life and is useful for some work. In short you have to sell Zerang.”

“But who wants to buy such a donkey?” asked Ali

“You don’t need to mention all the problems of your donkey when you want to sell it” said Mullah. “Take him in front of the Bazaar where there are lots of people going in and out of the Bazaar and the nearby Masjed (Mosque). You get a placard in your hand with a few words to attract attention. You clearly have to state the qualities of your donkey.” said Mullah.

“What qualities?” asked Ali

“Tell how loving he is, he never gets angry, he is intelligent, quick to react and he is extremely loyal and sensitive to how his owner feels. For instance, tell the would-be interested buyer, when Zerang feels that you cannot run, he stops running and slows down, he is economical and very good natured. Also, he yells often when you the owner is in danger of being run over by these things called automobiles, or being attacked by a thief.”

“But Mullah what you say is not true, how can you ask me to lie?” asked Ali “My donkey is so exhausted after a day’s work that I almost need to carry him home,” pointed out Ali.

“Of course, these are true, but you don’t know what is going on in Zerang’s head, and what he feels. It *may* be that he feels that there is a danger ahead and acts by yelling or even passing urine at a most unexpected time and place to warn you,” said Mullah. “As for you carrying your donkey home in the evening, I think is a very noble of you to do so. But also, it is a generous gesture by Zerang to let you express your appreciation of the work he is doing for you," continued the Mullah.

Ali thanked Mullah and went straight to the front of the Bazaar with Zerang.

Ali had a great success in his pitch in demonstrating the qualities of his animal, as instructed by Mullah; he had several offers by people who wanted to pay a good price for Zerang.

As an old friend of Mullah, Ali was supposed to go to the Friday prayers and tell the result of the venture. So, he did. Ali went to the Friday prayers with a smiling face and, after the usual service, Mullah approached him and was sure that Ali had very good news on the sale of his animal. He asked Ali, "How did you get on?"

"Very well," said Ali

"Did you get a good price for Zerang?" asked Mullah.

"No, because I did not sell Zerang" replied Ali.

"Why not? Did you not have any offers?" asked Mullah.

"Of course – plenty," said Ali

"Then why did you not sell it?"

"You see your honour, I went as you directed to the Bazaar and stood outside beside my donkey, holding a placard, just as you instructed. There was then a crowd of people gathering around me and I started to tell them about the qualities of Zerang as you had asked me to do. In fact, I had learnt and recited what you had said to me word by word.

What followed was that the crowd of people around me were all convinced about the qualities of this wonderful donkey, and so was I. I, therefore, asked myself why I should not buy this wonderful and good donkey myself?" And when I realized that I don't need to pay anything for it, I was sure that I had a bargain."

Mullah then asked Ali to recite what he has been telling the crowd and said: "You are absolutely right, Ali. If I did not have such a wonderful donkey myself, listening to you I would have offered to buy Zerang[5] from you and I would have given you a good price for it."

"My Donkey is so exhausted after a day's work that I need to carry him home."

---

5 Zerang in Farsi means a clever, quick minded individual with rapid reactions.

The Barber of Masjed-e-Shah (King's Mosque)

In the 1940s, my secondary school – Dar ul Fonoon – was situated near the top of Nasserieh/Nasser Khosro Street. A kilometre or so down the street from my school was Sabzeh Maidan and the Grand Bazaar of Tehran, almost inseparable from Masjed-e-Shah – the King's Mosque. Some days, at midday, a few of my class mates and I used to walk down the street to grab a snack for lunch outside the Bazaar where one could find an enormous choice, such as bread with cheese, grapes or other fruits or a skewer of Kebab with Barbarie Nan – a type of Persian bread. Then we used to sit on a low stone wall in front of the Masjed-e-Shah and observe the people and traders around the Bazaar. A friend of mine was a fantastic cartoonist and used to sketch people or things which he found unusual, comical or interesting. As a musician I always had a book of musical staves and noted the tunes played by a musician playing a Kamancheh – a stringed instrument with 3 or 4 strings, a finger board, tuning pegs and a belly covered by a goat skin. The instrument stands on the floor and is played with a bow.

Outside the Bazaar there was a variety of street traders and a number of interesting people within a mini-shop or behind a stall; these traders would open early in the morning and close in the evening when day's end was announced by the sun and through the Minareh of the mosque calling for the evening prayer.

The following comes from my diaries and personal memories of some of the interesting people whom one could see.

One of the regular fixtures in the Bazaar – Masjed eh Shah

complex was a middle aged barber with a well trimmed beard. He had a red coloured beard, which nicely covered his cheeks and chin. In fact, most of his face, other than his nose and eyes, were covered by his beard, which he was undoubtedly using henna to enhance. He looked confident and, when he was not shaving people or cutting hair, he used to sing to attract attention; at intervals he would shout, reminding people to shave or trim beards before entering the mosque. A curious thing about this guy was that he had bottles of liquid on benches around him; he would say that he had the formula of an elixir formulated by Ibn Sina (Avicenna) in the 10th century and that it had a magical effect on the growth of beards, such as his own. The fact that his head was bald was irrelevant, either to his sales tactics or to people who bought this elixir.

The first time I identified him in the crowd of the traders, I noted that he had two baskets beside him with walnuts in their shell. I was rather curious to know what a barber was doing with walnuts beside him.

By coincidence, he had the same kind of setup as the shoe cleaner who was trading beside him, which consisted of a chair for the customers to sit on, a kind of makeshift table on which was placed a copper tray with a brush and clipper and also a metal shaving mug.

We students discussed this amongst ourselves and hypothesised what the two baskets of walnuts had to do with trimming beards or cutting hair.

We returned to the area several times, but we still did not notice any sign that the nuts were actually broken; in any case, there was nothing to crack the shells with and there were no broken shells anywhere. Nor was anyone buying them. The only thing was that the total number of the walnuts in the 2 baskets every day seemed the same but there was a different number of nuts in the individual baskets. It was interesting that during the time that we were observing our barber, usually around midday, people who were entering the Masjed were going in for midday prayers; most of these only sat on the barber's chair for a brief period to have their beards trimmed.

The puzzle went on for weeks until the day that the Minister of Commerce came to visit the Bazaar one Thursday. On that day, a couple of friends and I decided to walk down as usual and get our lunch near the Bazaar. At this time, there were a few young people queuing to have a shave. The mystery became clarified.

The barber was putting a walnut in the mouth of a customer, between his cheek and teeth, thus stretching the skin to get a closer shave on the skin of the cheeks. He would first take a walnut from the right basket and put it in the right-hand side of the mouth between the cheek and the teeth, before moving the walnut to the left-hand side of the mouth to shave this side. Once he had shaved both sides of the face, he would take the used walnut out of the mouth and put it in the left-hand side basket. It now became clear as to why there were walnuts in the two baskets; one for the unused, clean walnuts and the second for the used walnuts in a different basket.

Hopefully, he would wash the walnuts at night before starting the next day, but no one was able to verify this.

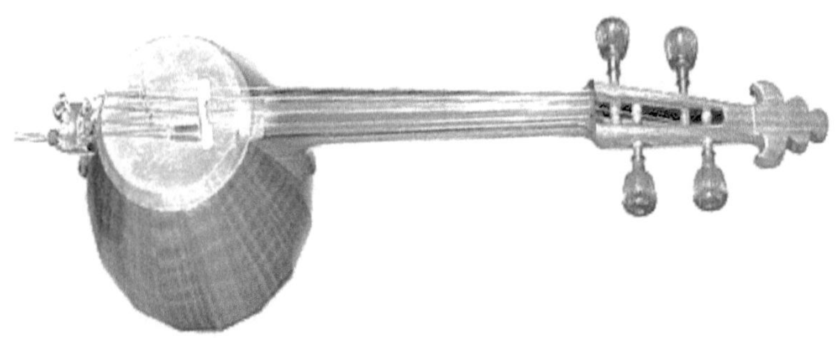

Kamancheh

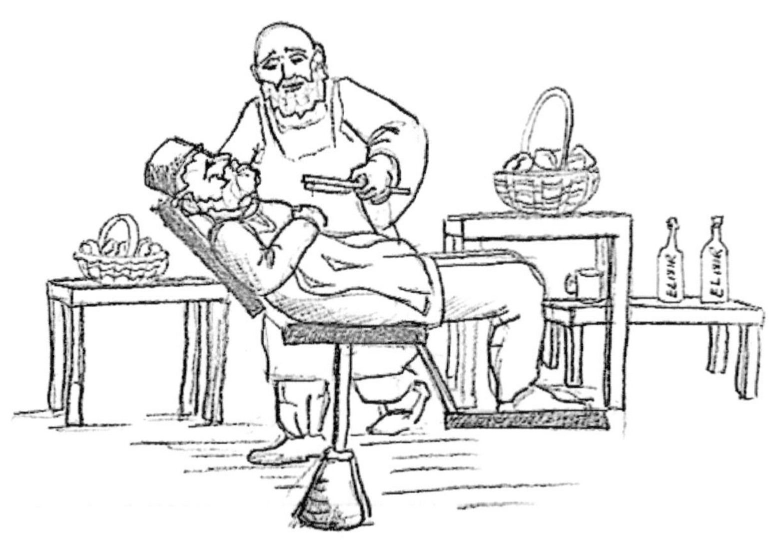

The Barber of Masjed-e-Shah
and his two walnut baskets

Chess Game in Suzhou

China and Persia, two of the greatest empires of the pre-Christian era in Asia, had important cultural and trade relationships going back to 500 BC.

During the Parthian and Sassanid dynasties in Persia and the Han and Tang dynasties in China, the relationship was flourishing.

However, during the Safavid Dynasty in Persia and at the tail end of the Ming Dynasty in China, the exchange of scientists, astronomers and artisans was at its peak.

During the reign of Shah Abbas the Great, at the end of 16th and beginning of 17th Centuries, many hundreds of Chinese were residing in Persia. Potters introduced glazed tiles and miniature painting in Isfahan and influenced Persian art and craft. In exchange the Persians introduced science and technology into China.

These co-operations apart, there were rivalries in many domains and the ambassadors of the two empires dealt with treaties and tried to bargain from the point of strength.

The following story was passed on to me by my granddad:

During the reign of Shah Abbas, a Persian Vizier was sent from Isfahan to China for a goodwill visit which, amongst other things, involved exchange of military and astronomical hardware and equipment.

Travel was tough and involved passing through areas ruled by bandits and warlords. Therefore, a division of the Persian army with supplies and water was to accompany the Vizier, as well as women and gold, to entice the Chinese and bring about a good 'deal'.

After three months of travel, the Vizier arrived to his meeting place in the city of Suzhou, in the east of China; at the time, this was the centre of culture, commerce and economy in the Empire of China. He was accommodated in the mansion reserved for foreign dignitaries. The Vizier had brought with him a variety of foodstuffs, such as lamb, poultry and rice. He could not, overtly, take wine but he secretly had several of his best horses carrying large pots of wine. He had chosen two of his best cooks, his wife, a number of slaves, servants and musicians in order to enjoy his diplomatic mission.

After a few days of rest, eating and having a good time, Ali-Agha-Isfahanie, the Vizier of Shah Abbas-e-Safavi, had the first of his meetings with his counterpart from the Empire of China.

It was on the third visit that the Ambassador of China asked if the Vizier would play a game of chess.

An enormous chess board was set in the room, with pawns as large as real soldiers. The Persian Vizier was led to the Chess Board where Zheng-Huang-Li-Bo-Li was waiting to meet him.

Before the game began, there was an exchange of presents: an exquisite silk carpet from the province of Kashan was the gift of the Persian Vizier, whilst Zheng-Huang-Li-Bo-Li presented a pair of Chinese vases, specially made and crafted for the occasion, to his Persian guest.

Now the real game began. For every move there was a pause and a proposal from the Persian and then a pause with a counter proposal by the Chinese, whilst he was making his move. It was all jovial and true to the oriental spirit – smiling and joking mixed with serious messages at every move.

Suddenly the Chinese stopped and said to the Persian,"I want to give you a Chinese puzzle, to see if you can solve it. Can I call you Ali for now, if I may?"

"Of course. I will try, Zheng," replied Ali.

The puzzle was propounded: "Imagine if ever there were to be a war between our two countries," he then clapped his hands three times, in quick succession. There upon, in walked a Chinese heavyweight champion wrestler, with a sack of rice over his shoulder. Zheng clapped his hands again once more. This time, the champion poured the contents of the sack over the chess board, overturning all the black and white pawns and completely covering the chessboard.

This was the Chinese puzzle.

"My dear Ali," said Zheng, "in case of conflict, consider your country as the chess board and these grains of rice as Chinese soldiers and military personnel. By their sheer number our soldiers can destroy and overwhelm the population of Persia and occupy every town, village and hamlet of your country. Well, my dear Ali, your move now," said Zheng triumphantly.

Ali, the Persian, lost no time in responding with his solution to the puzzle.

He quickly clapped his hands three times. A slim, Persian eunuch entered the room, carrying two roosters, one under each arm; they were moving their hungry heads in their characteristic manner in search of food.

'What on earth is this?' wondered the Chinese.

He was amazed and amused as to how this Persian Vizier was going to solve the puzzle.

Ali clapped his hands once more, signalling the servant to let go of the roosters. They fluttered down onto the board.

Immediately, they started picking up the rice from the chess board, eating the grains mouthful after mouthful. This was obviously the solution to Zheng's puzzle.

"You see my dear Zheng, we don't have a big army in Persia, as you have in China, but we would manage to get rid of your army just the same."

The Chess game was never finished but Ali and Zheng remained friends all their lives.

Addendum: In 2013 I was for 10 days in China and visited Suzhou and some of its delightful villages. I had the opportunity to tell the above story to my friend Xuili Wong, a Professor of Dermatology in Shanghai, one of my hosts, who took me to Suzhou. See photo below.

View of the Garden of the Stately Home in Suzhou where the foreign emissaries and Guests were accommodated.

Hakob and the Simurgh; A Christmas tale

This is a story of a Persian boy called Hakob, about 400 years ago. He was born to an Armenian family in the city of Tabriz, within the province of Azerbaijan, during the reign of a great Persian king, Shah Abbas I of Safavid Dynasty. Hakob never knew his father; he had been Choirmaster of the local church but had died in an earthquake, when his mother, Miriam, was 4 months pregnant.

At the time, the Armenians were the largest minority in Azerbaijan, and were usually recognized and protected by the Persian kings. However, the area was a disputed territory between the Empire of Persia and that of the Ottomans. The Armenians were always under threat when the administration changed and the area fell under the authority of fundamentalist Islamic rulers of Ottomans, since Armenians are Christians of the Eastern Church, which originated in the missions of the Apostles Bartholomew and Thaddeus in the 1st century.

When Hakob was born, Mariam became a single mother and was helped by the church with provision of work and accommodation in a Nunnery and, for the next five years. Mariam and Hakob had a modest but stable life.

The Christians of Tabriz were a close-knit community, in which people looked after one another. This was particularly the case when their rulers were keen to enforce the Islamic rules, which allowed Moslems to take advantage of the Armenians, who could be imprisoned and enslaved. By the time Hakob was 5, he was in the church choir and was well known for his voice, which received great praise from the Priest and congregation. This also provided him and his mother with small amount of extra cash for singing on Sundays and special occasions like Christmas.

Like most Persian children, at the age of 5, Hakob was introduced to stories about the legendary bird, the 'Simurgh', which had a reputation of being sensitive, with supernatural strength; she could fly at the edge of the sky, far above the earth. Simurgh had the power to cure the incurables and was always ready to help those in desperate need. No wonder that many vulnerable and sensitive young children found, in Simurgh, a friend.

One Sunday during early autumn, when the trees were shedding their yellow and brown leaves, Hakob was walking home from the church service, kicking the leaves just like any little boy, playing to pass the time between school and home. He saw something unusual within the mass of leaves. This did not look like any autumn leaf but more like a feather, with a most outstanding multicolour pattern, like a rainbow. He kicked at the feather which rose into the air. From nowhere came a thunderous noise; a tornado whipped up and terrific lightening uprooted trees and burnt the shrubs at the side of the road. Hakob, in panic, ran for cover. Cowering, he turned back to look. In the midst of the chaos, he saw a colossal, bird-like creature landing.

"Don't run Hakob, you need not be frightened, the feather you kicked into the air was mine, I thought you needed me." Hakob at once knew that this was no other being but the Simurgh.

"I have been watching you for some time now and I know

the plight of your mother," said the Simurgh. She then handed a few more of her feathers to Hakob and said, "Keep these feathers; put them in a small bag, attach them to a string and put the string round your neck. Should the occasion arise that you need a little help, take one of the feathers and let it fly in the air."

"Excuse me Simurgh, where do you live and how can you come quickly to my help?" asked Hakob.

The Simurgh then started: "I'll try to explain.

Look ... far away, you see some mountains, if you continue on your right-hand side, many miles away you reach a very tall mountain which is called Damavand, there you can find a special tree – a "Gaokerena". That is where I live."

Hakob did not quite understand but said, "Thank you Simurgh."

"I'll tell you what," said Simurgh, "would you like me to take you to see where I live?"

"Well, I would love to, but my mother is waiting for me and she will worry if I'm late," replied Hakob

"Don't worry about the time, it only takes a moment; you will be home in no time," replied the bird.

Simurgh bent her neck and asked Hakob to sit astride. Into the air she flew, faster than light.

Hakob could neither see nor remember the journey, it was so quick. In no time he was on the top of the world. Now he could clearly see miniature cities and trees from the top of the Damavand peak, and he saw the "Gaokerena Tree" and the nest of the Simurgh. Then he was told by Simurgh to close his eyes. When he opened them a second later, he recognised the walls of the Nunnery which was his home. He could not believe it!

He arrived home full of excitement, asking his mother if she had heard of the Alborz mountain and a tree called "Gaokerena?"

Before his mother had a chance to respond he said: "Maman," as he called his mother. "I have a ridden on the neck of Simurgh to the Damavand peak and back today!"

"Are you all right Hakob? You don't make sense, my child," replied Mariam.

"It is true, look she gave me a bunch of her feathers too," said Hakob.

"Don't be silly, come and eat and let's do some of your work for the choir," said his mother, "And don't take those dirty feathers to bed."

For the first time Hakob disobeyed his mother; he was not going to separate the Simurgh's feathers from his body. He put the feathers into a small bag and he attached the bag to the copper chain to which was fixed the Armenian Cross given to him by his grandmother.

He went to bed, dreaming about what had happened; he never forgot the experience.

Hakob in Ardabil

In the year 1606, barely 6 years old, Hakob and his family became the victims of the Turkish Ottoman and the Persian Shah Abbas's war; they had been fighting for about 3 years and the war was going to last for another 12 years.

Partially in the way of protection, the Shah took the drastic decision to deport Armenian residents in the Persian part of Azerbaijan from their homeland to Isfahan, which had become the capital city of the country. The deportation involved almost

500,000 men, women and children. Some were transported by horses and carts, camels, donkeys or mules. Others had to walk. There were rivers to cross and rough terrain to climb; this was difficult for the very young, old and infirm. Many never reached their destination in an area in the perimeter of Isfahan called "New Julfa" and villages around which became known as "Bourvari."

This deportation was in fact an act of mercy, relieving the Armenian community in Azerbaijan from the continuing ethnic cleansing by the Turks who were threatening their lives and livelihood by imprisonment and slavery because of their faith. Nevertheless, the move, which was assisted by Shah Abbas' army, was traumatic; it resulted in considerable loss of life and disruption of the community. Many people died by drowning in crossing the rivers, by fatigue or by falling from narrow passages into ravines of the mountainous terrain. Some families lost their children; other members of a family were separated and lost, presumed dead. In one instance, whilst people were crossing a stream, a freak storm and flash flood caught animals and their riders by surprise, causing havoc. The gentle flow of the stream turned into a rapid running river which swept away animals, people and their belongings. This happened early in October, with the weather turning icy cold.

Hakob was sitting in front of his mother, riding on a mule. They were caught up by the storm whilst they were crossing, what should have been, a shallow stream – it became a deep river. Despite the fact that, usually, mules are sturdy and safe animals to ride in mountain passes or on rough terrain, the animal stumbled and fell, throwing Hakob and his mother into

Hakob became entangled in the branch
of a large tree, he was unconscious but alive

the fast running water. They were swept and dragged away separately with nothing to hold on.

Hakob lost consciousness but, by chance, became entangled in branches of a large tree which was floating on the swollen river. Although he was saved, he remained unconscious.

Days later, Hakob regained consciousness; he found himself in bed, in a warm room with a wood fire glowing. There was a white-bearded old man sitting beside the bed. On the wall, apart from a couple of hanging carpets, there were pictures of the prophet Mohammed and some Arabic writing, indicating that this was a house belonging to a Moslem family.

Hakob was petrified at the thought that he was probably imprisoned to be used as a slave. Some Moslems, especially from Turkish Ottoman, had a reputation of treating Armenians and Jews in an appalling way at that time. He tried to sit. The thought occurred to him to make use of one of Simurgh's feathers to seek help. But the chain on which his cross and the bag of feathers were attached was not around his neck.

Hakob regained consciousness, finding himself in a bed with an old man sitting beside him.

"Where am I, where is my mother and where is my chain?" he screamed.

Now the old man came and put his arm round Hakob's shoulder and said, "Do not fear child, you are in a safe place. I am Sheikh Ali Hossein and no one is going to harm you in my house."

The Sheikh then called his wife, Zobaideh Khanum, and his grandson Hassan, to come.

"He is awake," he said, "We have a miracle in our house." Hassan rushed to the room first and, with a beaming smile, jumped on the bed saying:

"I am Hassan, I am 6. I am so pleased to have you here as I have no brother to play with."

"Where am I?" whispered Hakob.

"You are here in our house," replied Hassan.

"No, I mean, which place, am I back in Tabriz?"

"No!" said Zobaideh Khanum, who now arrived in the room carrying a tray of bread, cheese and tea. "You had better eat something before anything else. Hassan, you go and get some clothes for this boy – we don't know your name, how do you call yourself?"

"I am Hakob, what is your name?" replied Hakob.

"I am called Zobaideh Khanum but you can call me Khanum."

Now Sheikh Ali-Hossain who had been sitting silently in the room said: "I am Sheikh Ali-Hossain; you may call me Sheikh Agha. You are in Ardabil. My son, who is a fisherman, found you by the side of the river in an uprooted tree. At first he thought you were not alive but he knew how to help to make you breathe and brought you home."

Agha Khan's son had been married but, six years ago; his wife had died during the delivery of twin sons, one of whom also died at birth. The other, Hassan, survived. So, Agha Khan, seeing a little boy the same age as his grandson brought home by his son, really thought that God had given him back the other twin.

Hakob slowly remembered that it was when he was on a mule crossing a river that, suddenly, he was swept away by a flood. He wanted to know where, exactly, he was by the side of the river and asked if he could go back to see if he could find his cross as he was Armenian Christian. He then realised that the people who had saved his life were Moslem and said: "I should not ask this because the cross does not mean anything to you."

"Hakob, you are a gift from God, and we will do anything we can to try to find your cross," said the Sheikh.

"How far is the riverbank where I was found?" asked Hakob.

"Not far; maybe an hour's walk on the banks of the Baliqly Chay River – the River of the many fishes," came the answer.

"Grandfather, can we go tomorrow to see if we can find Hakob's Cross?" asked Hassan.

"I have a better idea," replied Sheikh Agha.

He said that he knew a very well known Armenian Priest, who was in charge of a little monastery.

"I think, if anyone found a Christian Cross, they would hand it to him, as the Muslims would not like such an object," he said.

The next day Sheikh Agha and the two boys set off to first walk along the bank of the river. They saw the tree in which Hakob was caught but no copper chain or cross was found.

Next they went to the friend of Sheikh Agha, Father Mardoustian but, again, no religious object had been handed over to him.

Hakob, Hassan and Sheikh Agha went every day for a week along the bank of the river and then to the priest with disappointing results.

Now Hakob was stuck; he accepted that his life was with Hassan and his family.

In December 1606, Hakob decided to let Hassan into the secret that his concern was not only the loss of his cross but also the loss of another important possession – the bag attached to the same chain – which contained the feather of the legendary Simurgh.

Before confessing to his friend Hassan, Hakob wanted a solemn assurance that Hassan would keep the secret and would not reveal it to anyone. They went first to a nearby Mosque and then to the Monastery. Each one put his left hand over the Quran in the Mosque and on the Bible in the Monastery and swore by the holy books to keep their secret to themselves. They decided to become spiritual brothers. Back home, Hassan and Hakob told Sheikh Agha of their decision to become brothers in God. Sheikh Agha was delighted; he told the whole family that he now had two grandsons.

There was no chance that Hakob could ever find his mother. However, he wanted to remain Armenian and continue to sing in the Monastery.

This was no problem for the Muslim family with whom he was living. In fact, from time to time, Hassan went with him to the Armenian Service and, occasionally, Hakob would go to the Mosque with Hassan.

It was interesting to see two little boys being friends and brothers and continuing with their respective faiths. It was most extraordinary that Hassan's family, totally devout Muslims, accepted this unusual alliance of the two boys.

The 6th January 1607 and the Armenian Christmas was approaching; there was nervousness in Hakob's new family as they were sure that the boy would miss his family, particularly his mother and grandmother.

They bought him a chain and an Armenian Cross that they gave to him on the 5th January, the day before the Armenian Christmas. This brought tears to the eyes of Hakob and the whole of Sheikh Agha's family.

That night, as Hakob went to bed, he knelt beside his bed with the cross in his hand and talked to Baba – Father Christmas.

"Dear Baba, I thank you for giving me a new Cross and thank you for giving me a new family, but I do miss my mother. Please give me back my mother, just for Christmas and also my Grandmother. I am so happy here; I never want to be separated from my brother Hassan."

He imagined for a moment that he was hugging his mother and thanked Baba for the lovely thought.

Tears of joy filled his eyes. He fell, happily asleep on the floor.

That night was a strange one; Hakob dreamed of Jesus, who was telling him that his mother had safely arrived at Isfahan, pleading with the king to find her son. Then the King issued an order to all his governors across the Persian Empire to do their utmost to find Hakob.

On Christmas day, the 6th of January Hakob woke up early. He still had his new cross and chain in his hand, but he felt, also, as though he had something – a chain – round his neck. He thought that he was still dreaming. But, no, he certainly wasn't dreaming. He remembered that he was once told by his grandmother that if he wanted to make sure that he was awake he could test it by pinching his bottom, so just to check, he pinched the side of his bottom; he definitely felt the pain. He was in no doubt that he really had a chain around his neck.

Sitting up, he felt his neck and there was the old copper chain given to him by his grandmother; attached to it was his original cross that he had lost during the river crossing. More wonderfully, there was the old money bag and the Simurgh Feathers within it.

He jumped out of bed and called Hassan.

"Look, look, I have my chain, the cross and the feathers."

"Go to sleep Hak," the nickname the family called Hakob.

"Come on, get up and see what Saint Nicholas has brought me," said the excited child, shaking Hassan to wake up.

Now Hassan jumped out of bed, catching the excitement. The boys had not realised that it was still dark and the family woke up wondering what was happening at that time of the night. Candles were soon lit and now the whole family was awake. Hakob started to explain about Simurgh.

Sheikh Agha said, "Of course I know about Simurgh. I never took notice of the so-called bird but some people have apparently seen it."

"Sheikh Agha, would you allow us to call Simurgh and see if she can take us to find my mother, that is Hassan and I?" asked Hakob.

"Where is your mother and how you are going to travel?" asked Sheikh Agha.

"Maybe she's in Isfahan, as the last time we were together she was heading that way with the Shah's soldiers. If the Simurgh comes she would know where to take us," replied Hakob.

"Look son, you're excited about Christmas, which we fully understand. We appreciate that at this time of the year you are missing your mother but, how on earth can you go to Isfahan which is at the end of the kingdom."

Hakob was at pains to explain and he was not sure whether the 'airing of a feather' of the Simurgh, would work, or if Simurgh would agree or even had the ability to transport him to Isfahan from Ardabil. However, he thought that the joy of seeing his mother was worth a try, even if unsuccessful.

“I don’t believe you can do it, Hakob, but yes, go ahead and dream away my son,” said Sheikh Agha.

Before Sheikh Agha had even finished his sentence, Hassan jumped in and said: “Grandfather, please let me go with my brother!”

Without further discussion the permission was granted.

Now Hakob loudly said: “My dear Simurgh, this is the time to show that you are the bird of your word and your reputation.”

Hakob gently took a feather from the bag around his neck and threw it out of the window into the dark sky. But the wind outside immediately blew it back into the room. After several attempts, he thought of an ingenious idea; the boys both took a deep breath in, and then forcefully blew the air out of their mouths. This provided the extra push necessary for the feather to stay outside before they closed the window. Now the whole of the family saw something that they could not believe.

Whilst the sky was totally black, they could see the feather, like a shooting star, was glowing and gradually disappearing from their sight into the dark of night.

Then the whole family waited; nothing happen for what seemed to be ages. In fact, after only a minute, the whole sky became alight like a sunny day. Suddenly, a giant beauty of a bird appeared in front of the window. This was, indeed, the Simurgh.

“Hakob, I am sorry I am late; I was helping a Caspian Tiger caught in the net of a nasty hunter on this holy night.

“We will stop for a few minutes to greet the tiger whilst we are travelling down towards Isfahan, to see your mother” said Simurgh.

"How did you know that we want to go to Isfahan, Simurgh?" asked Hassan.

"I know, as that is where Hakob's mother is and the idea is to get there in time for Christmas service."

"Are you a Christian Simurgh," asked Hassan.

"I have no religion but work for God and the good of God, to help those in need," replied Simurgh.

Hakob and Hassan were about to mount on the back of Simurgh when Sheikh Agha asked them to wait a moment. He went and removed a beautiful Ardabil silk carpet which was hanging on the wall and put it on the back of Simurgh for the children to sit on and then present to Mariam for Christmas.

Simurgh and the children said farewell to Sheikh Agha and went on their way.

Travel to Isfahan

Simurgh asked the children to hold tight; they snuggled under her feathers to keep warm. She reminded them that she wanted to call to see her friend the Caspian tiger and his little family on their way.

In less than a minute Simurgh landed in clearing in a forest; she approached a huge terrifying-looking tiger, his cubs and the tigress.

Hakob and Hassan were at first frightened and would not move. This was until the tiger came toward Simurgh, carrying one of the cubs in its mouth, to greet their visitors. Then, suddenly, from behind the big trees, a fox jumped out, dancing around.

Hakob and Hassan were, again anxious thinking that the fox was trying to steal the cub and that the tiger would turn and savage the fox.

"Children don't be afraid," said Simurgh, feeling their fear. "Here in this beautiful forest, only hunters are the enemies of these wild animals. Hunters kill tigers, foxes and other animals for fun. Some hunters even collect the head of the animal to hang on the wall as they would a silk carpet as an ornament; it is supposed to show their heroism, which is pathetic."

This calmed the children who got down from the back of Simurgh to see more closely the family of the Caspian tiger. In no time, many other animals made their entry to the area. A tall, handsome deer showing off his branched horns arrived, followed by a wild pig, a female deer, a pack of wolves and a great variety of other animals. One of the last to join was a slow-moving bear, before a flying cavalcade of birds in hundreds flew over the area before displaying themselves on the branches of the trees. A cheeky monkey was not going to miss the show and made her presence heard by her typical 'wobble', no doubt trying to draw attention to its little one on her back.

They all gathered to greet Simurgh.

The boys were fascinated and amazed and, gradually, so amused that they forgot the purpose of the journey. However, Simurgh soon reminded all that the visit was just to greet her friend and his family. She promised to get back to the forest for the 'Now-Ruz' – the Persian New Year on 21 March, when she could stay a bit longer.

The boys climbed once more on to her back and resumed their travel.

Simurgh flew the boys over many cities, forests, rivers, high mountains and deserts, always high above the clouds; the two little passengers at times imagined that they were sitting on the clouds. At other times, when there was no cloud, they had a bird's eye view of the land below.

In what felt like no time, Simurgh asked them to hold tight as she was descending below the cloud. She explained that they would soon be flying over a hill on which there was the Zoroastrian Fire Temple. This marked their impending arrival at their destination, the New Jufal, which was a village built for deported Armenians, within the district of Isfahan.

Hakob's excitement was almost uncontainable, asking questions without giving a chance to Simurgh to answer. The most important were, did Simurgh know that his mother was alive and how did she know the whereabouts of his mother?

"I know that your mother is alive, and we are heading towards where she is right now. In fact, we will see her soon" replied Simurgh.

"I have no doubt that she will be in a new Monastery Church called Vank or the Holy Saviour Cathedral, you may get down at the back of the Church; you enter the church from the front door. You will see your mother kneeling in front of the Alter where there is an Icon of Jesus. She is wearing a black net scarf over her head, which you will recognise. This is the scarf which was given to her by the priest when your father died, and you have seen her wearing it on many occasions at church celebrations when you were singing in the Choir in Tabriz. Put on this robe and go and sing with the Choristers; a place is reserved for you." Simurgh then handed over a choir boy's robe and added, "The carpet from Sheikh Agha will be hung on the wall of your mother's room when you get home with her."

"What do you want to do Hassan? If you want to go back to your home in Ardabil I shall take you back," Simurgh asked Hassan.

Now Hassan had a problem; he neither wanted to leave Hakob nor be without his family in Isfahan. The Simurgh saw the anguish in the eye of the little Hassan and said.

"If you wish, you may stay for a few days with Hakob; have these feathers and, when you want to return, let me know by 'airing a feather', she suggested kindly, before handing over a few of her feathers to Hassan. She told him that if he went into the church to stand beside other children, he would be welcomed.

Simurgh said farewell and flew away.

Hakob and Hassan entered the Church and did exactly as Simurgh had asked them to do. Hakob recognised his mother straight away. Despite a tremendous urge to run towards her mother, Hakob went to the place reserved for him. Hassan also went and stood beside other children in the church.

The Priest asked the people to stand and pray for the blessings they had received during the year. He then asked the choir to sing the Christmas Hymn and the congregation to join the refrains.

Mariam instantly recognised Hakob's voice, with its unique tonal quality; she turned towards the choir, whispering to her mother who was standing beside her.

"Mother, God has given us back my child." The Priest then addressed the congregation.

"Dear God, we thank you for the special day when you offered your son to save us. Today you gave our sister Mariam back her child, Hakob. We pray especially for the Moslem family who protected Hakob and we welcome Hassan the brother of Hakob into our midst.

Almighty God, grant us the *Oneness of Humanity and Unity in Diversity."*

The Service ended and now Hakob and Mariam could be united. But Hakob had something to do first; he had to find Hassan and then to see his mother.

At last Mariam could feel the heartbeat of her son on her breast by lifting and hugging Hakob. She did the same with Hassan and they walked home hand in hand, one boy on each side.

Simurgh, yet again true to her word, took Hassan back to Ardabil a few days later.

This was not however the end of the history of Hakob and Hassan. Simurgh provided them, twice every year, a re-union of brothers; at Christmas in Isfahan and Now-Ruz in Ardabil until the year 1618 AD.

In 1618, the 15 years of the Ottoman-Persian war ended and Hakob and Hassan, now young men, formed a joint business enterprise. Hakob and Hassan Trading Company, for import and export was founded.

In the year 1619 Hassan moved to Isfahan for good.

A year later Hassan's father, after so many years of solitude, married Mariam, Hakob's mother. By the blessing of the King, Shah Abass, the marriage was authorised and registered in the Armenian Church as well as Masjed eh Shah – the King's Mosque.

Sheikh Agha Khan's family also moved to Isfahan. A big and multi-faith family was now established.

Just a little 'window of hope for Unity in Diversity'.

Exterior view of the Holy Saviour Cathedral in New JULFA.[6]

The Holy Saviour Cathedral above (Armenian: also known as the Church of the Saintly Sisters) is a cathedral located in the New Julfa district of Isfahan, Iran. It is commonly referred to as the "Vank" which means monastery or convent.

The cathedral was established in 1606 for hundreds of thousands of Armenian deportees who came to Iran during the Ottoman war.

[6] Picture by Rasool abbasi17 - Own work, CC BY-SA 4.0, https://commons.wikimedia.org/w/index.php?curid=37740823

Kambuz and the Tigris (*Dajleh*)

There is a well known adage in Farsi, the Persian language: 'Do a good deed, even if it is as insignificant as throwing a piece of bread into the Dajleh, so that God will reward you when you are stranded in the desert.' This apparently arose from an old Persian tale:

When the Persian Empire was ruled by the great King Darius, around 500 BC, there was a man called Kambuz who, every morning at dawn, walked on the bank of the river Tigris to his work on a farm. At a particular point on his walk, near the area where the Tigris and Euphrates join to form Shat al Arab before running into the Persian Gulf, Kambuz would stop, meditate for a couple of minutes and throw a loaf of bread into the water. He was a private man and religious, a Zardoshti or Zoroastrian; and in his mind he was doing something good each day.

Time went by and during one Now-Ruz – the beginning of the Persian calendar (21st March) – Kambuz decided to take a holiday, which involved passing through the Sahara Desert. Unfortunately, in the middle of nowhere, there arose a sandstorm. Everything flew into the air or was buried in the sand; camel, food, water and bedding, all gone. Kambuz just about survived. When the storm settled, he considered how he could get out of the dreaded Sahara. Maybe he should start walking towards the north using the sun as his guide. But there was a mist of sand, making walking impossible. He struggled to find his way out of the blinding mist and, after a few minutes, he could see his footprints indicating that he was going round in circles and getting nowhere.

The heat was unbearable; thirst and the blazing sun on his body was drying him to death. Alone and desperate he put his hands together and began to say his last prayer. He called upon Ahura-Mazda, his God, to forgive his sins and purify his soul.

There came a deafening voice, reverberating through the air.

"KAMBUZ, KAMBUZ, THIS IS AHURA-MAZDA CALLING YOU. LOOK AROUND YOU".

Kambuz looked around. Amazed, he saw that the mist was lifting. The clouds gathered and the rain started to fall, cooling his body. He could now see an oasis through the mist, just a short distance away; there were trees and a camel was kneeling, with all of his possessions loaded and another standing for him to sit on.

Kambuz could now see an oasis through the mist, just a short distance away; there were trees and a camel was kneeling, with all of his possessions loaded and another standing for him to sit on.

He thought this to be a mirage and cried, "Thank you, Ahura-Mazda, for making me happy before I die by letting me see this beautiful mirage."

"Kambuz my child," came the reply, "This is not a mirage, it is real."

With a shaking voice Kambuz said, "Thank you Ahura-Mazda; why are you so merciful to your servant?"

"Kambuz, this is your deserved reward for feeding my fishes in the Tigris river for so many years. You have cared for my fishes; I am saving you in return... a fair exchange! I do not forget a good deed, even one as seemingly insignificant as throwing a loaf of bread into the Dajleh."

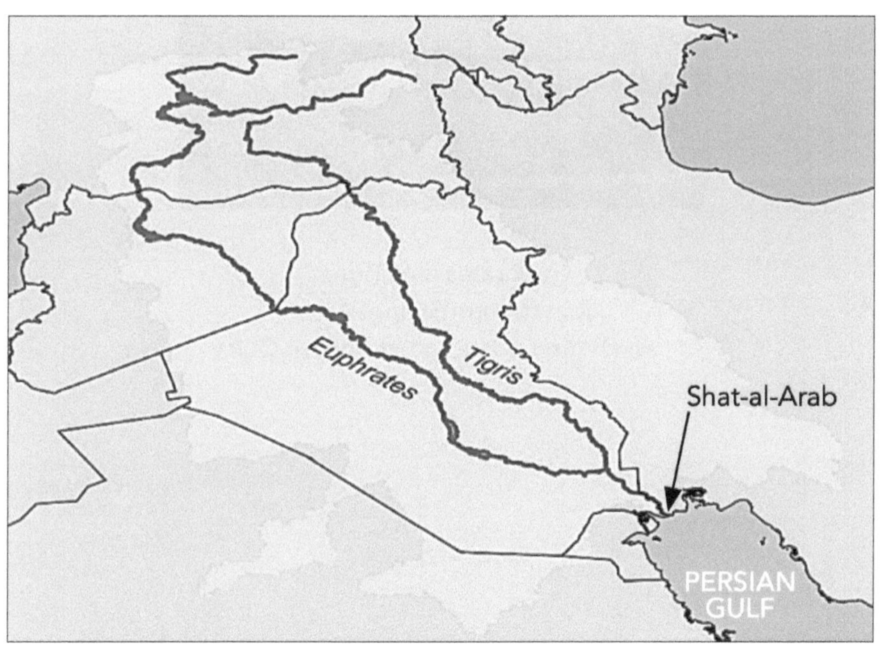

Shat-al-Arab in the Persian Gulf

Euphrates and Tigris
join to form Shat-al-Arab
which discharges to the Persian Gulf

Mephistopheles Tom

Once upon a time there was a community of mice, living in their traditional tunnel. They were in a state of siege because of one nasty cat called Mephistopheles – Mephistos for short.

Mephistos was not only dangerous to mice but also a bully towards small, female cats, from whom he expected obedience and submission.

Every morning Mephistos would sharpen his claws and wait outside the tunnel where the mice had burrowed. He would eat fat mouse, thin mouse, little mouse, big mouse, white mouse and black mouse – any mouse. The little ones, he liked to play with before putting his nasty teeth through their tender meat.

Fortunately, the mice had a very acute sense of hearing and a refined sense of smell; they could detect the tomcat at the end of the tunnel and they had built a number of escape routes. They had, also, succeeded to carve some replica mice in the hope that Mephistos would try to swallow a wooden mouse and choke. But Mephistos soon discovered the trick and took revenge by hiding outside the tunnel for hours, before pouncing on young mice which were adventurous or playful enough to forget the warning of their elders.

The mice were fairly inventive in taking revenge on Mephistos. One of their ways was to make a large, deep hole and cover it with a thin layer of soil. Then, if Mephistos tried to pounce on an agile mouse that accepted the risk of sitting on the roof of these trap caves eating a nut, the cat would fall deep into the hole with the roof of the trap over him. The mouse had to be quick and agile to escape injury from the soil on the roof of the cave and also from the sharp claws of Mephistos.

Things came to a head when a little mouse became the victim of Mephistos, who thought to play with the little mouse and use the game as an appetiser. The little mouse was injured but saved by the heroic action of another of the mice, who decided to take on the bullying cat. He was known in the community of mice as Moushang. Seeing the injured baby mouse, he scurried out of the tunnel; he boldly jumped on the back of Mephistos and bit the right ear of the beast. For a second, Mephistos had to let go of the little mouse, which he was passing from one paw to the other, in order to deal with Moushang. Mephistos lost his prey and the little mouse escaped; so did Moushang, who grabbed the little baby and carried it below into the tunnel. More than anything else, following this incident Mephistos lost the authority and respect of his own peers.

Now, the mouse community decided they were tired of the constant vigilance and of being prisoners in their tunnel. They decided that the time had arrived to do something radical with Mephistos and one or two kittens that he was trying to teach the art of hunting. Mephistos' speciality was to play with young mice and wait for the mother to leave the shelter to save the little things; instead she fell victim to the beast.

The mice held a meeting of the elders, in the presence of the heroes amongst them.

On the agenda for discussion and decision was one item; *How to deal with the tom effectively and keep the little ones safe.*

The 11 members of the council, wearing their official robes and hats, were gathered. Moushang, as the Mouse-

The Council of Mice

Chair declared the meeting open. Proposal and counter proposal poured in. One suggestion was that lame mice in the colony could be put out of the tunnel at the disposal of Mephistos, as a kind of offering, so that he left other mice in peace. One young mouse talked passionately about survival, stating that it would be normal to sacrifice the old and disabled for the benefit of those who could work for the good of the community.

One of the wise older councillors spoke eloquently; he reminded the Council that disabled mice are already at a disadvantage through no fault of their own. It would be reprehensible to put such defenceless creatures, who could not even run, at the disposition of the all-powerful cat. The wise mouse ended his speech by saying that: "the community which ignores its responsibilities towards the old and infirm cannot be considered as a community, let alone a caring society."

So, this proposal was categorically turned down by the majority as totally unacceptable.

Another suggestion was to try to mislead the kittens by getting the fastest-running mice to lead them towards an area where there were birds of prey, such as eagles. This would divert Mephistos' and the other cats' attention from the mice and, hopefully, the kittens would become prey to birds. This, too, was also rejected as the process would endanger those mice which were engaged in the distraction.

The best suggestion, which received overwhelming approval, was from a mouse who had studied the behaviour of cats; he realised that mice have a keen sense of hearing. The suggestion was that a bell, on a piece of string, should be placed around Mephistos' neck so that any slight movement would make the bell to ring and it would be heard by the mice. The suggestion was considered as an intelligent and innovative proposal. This motion became an approved decision and the Chair-Mouse declared the motion passed.

Then ... a little mouse in the back row asked, "Dear friends and fellow citizens, may I ask you a question?"

"No, sit down," many of the mice shouted.

The 'Sage' mouse asked the assembly to let him proceed to ask his question.

"Thank you Sage," said the little mouse continuing, "which one of us is going to hang this bell around the neck of Mephistos and how?"

There was a silence...Moushang as the Chair-Mouse asked: "Does anyone volunteer?"

Silence reigned.

The Chair-Mouse now said, "For now, we will keep the approved proposal on the Statute Book for further consideration when we can implement it."

The Sage-Mouse then said, "Maybe we should try to negotiate with Mephistos."

Mice shouted, "How can you negotiate with a born mouse killer like Mephistos?"

"You can always negotiate with enemies. We should remind ourselves that he may be persuaded to play with us to enhance his appetite; he could then try to eat different things than our children. We should understand that we are part of his living and should be more patient," said a pacifist mouse.

No agreement was reached.

Many years later Mephistos became blind. This was when Moushang volunteered to put the bell around his neck. Mephistos heard Moushang approaching but could not determine from which direction. Suspecting what was happening, he said to Moushang.

"You don't need to place a bell around my neck, just put it around your tail so that I can hear and follow you. You can, thus, protect me from being devoured by hungry foxes."

Moushang put the bell around its tail which was gripped by Mephistos to guide him.

This was a deal which led to a long lasting peace in the Kingdoms of the Cats and the Mice.

The moral of the story is that, *The Future has its own Twist.*

Mephistos following mouse with bell

Mullah Nasr al-Din and his Cat

It was during one of the Now-Ruz (Persian New Year) festivities that Mullah Nasr al-Din unexpectedly met an old friend in a shop where they were both buying a plant of 'Sonbol' (hyacinth), a specific flower for the Now-Ruz table. It had been a long time since they had seen one another, so there was a bit of hesitation before Mullah Nasr al-Din said, "Is that you Akbaz?" – a nickname for Mullah Akbar Aziz.

"Bless my soul; it is Nasrad" – the nickname for Mullah Nasr al-Din.

In fact, the friendship of these Mullahs went back to their student days when they were learning the verses of the Quran in their Madresseh.

Mullah Nasr al-Din was delighted with this chance encounter; he thought it would be a marvellous occasion to invite his friend for lunch at his home on Friday. They could have a bite to eat and take the chance to catch up, after a visit to the Mosque for the usual prayers.

He remembered that, as young Talabehs (Islamic theology students) when they were in the city of Qum, once a week they used to go to a famous restaurant called "Hajji Hossein-eh Shish Kababi" for a treat; they would eat the best polo-kabab (rice and kebab) in the city.

With this in mind, he thought that for Friday lunch he would ask Fatimeh, his wife, to prepare a polo-kabab for them to eat and they could reminisce about the halcyon days of their youth.

He hurried to his usual butcher's shop and bought 4 kg of

the best cut of lamb meat for the kabab. Full of joy of the Now-Ruz, Mullah jumped on his donkey and dashed home.

Fatimah, his wife, questioned him as to why he had bought so much meat, to which Mullah responded joyfully about meeting and inviting his old friend Akbar for lunch on Friday.

However, fate would intervene and there was a bit of problem with the lunch as planned by Mullah Nasr al-Din. For some time, Fatimah had had a lover; Mansoor, a young student of Mullah who often visited the house, especially when Fatimah was alone. As it happened, Mullah had to go away on Thursday – the day before the Friday that he had invited Akbaz for lunch. Fatimah began to cook the meal ready for Friday lunch. She got the lamb ready for the kabab and also half cooked the "polo".

"Don't forget to buy some Sumac," shouted Fatimah, just before Mullah Nasr al-Din left the house.

So, on Thursday, Fatimah, as was the usual practice, partially prepared the polo, by boiling the rice but leaving it half cooked, to complete cooking on the Friday. She also seasoned and prepared the meat for the kebab, ready to put on skewers and cook over the charcoal fire for completion as a kind of barbecue. In this way the meal for Friday was practically ready, needing only an hour or so to cook before being served on the day.

Unexpectedly, however, Mansoor arrived at the house near midday on Thursday and Fatimah asked him to stay for lunch, which he willingly agreed to. Soon Mansoor and Fatimah had a delicious meal – and more – which they thoroughly enjoyed.

Come Friday, the two Mullahs went to prayer at a nearby Mosque, after which they rode their donkeys to Mullah Nasr al-Din's house for lunch.

After the traditional washing of hands with Golab – rosewater – the usual greetings and the traditional presentation of a pot of honey by the guest to Fatimah, the two Mullahs proceeded to the dining room and sat down for lunch. They had the "Mezzeh" (hors d'oeuvre) of aubergine dip, after which they eagerly expected the main course to be served. But there was no smell of kabab; the smell of kabab would have usually been noticeable for miles to stimulate the stomach. So they waited impatiently for their main course; in the meantime they continued to eat Noon-o Panir va Sabzi (naan bread, white cheese and green vegetables), which should have been for the after meal, and drank "dough" (yoghurt drink).

After a long wait, Fatimah came into the dining room, with a dish of polo – but no kabab.

"Unfortunately," she sheepishly explained, "the cat has eaten the meat intended for the Kabab.

"Where is the cat?" enquired Mullah.

"In the kitchen," replied Fatimah who added, "please don't hurt her".

"Of course, I am not going to hurt the cat!" said Mullah Nasr al-Din;

He now showed his true genius by fetching their big kitchen scales and weighed the cat.

The weight of the cat was 2 kg. Mullah Nasr al-Din was then reflective and said: "I wonder how a cat weighing 2 kg, could have eaten 4 kg meat?"

A shocked Fatimah had no explanation!!

“Mullah you are the clever one, I am sure you will find the answer.”

“Of course,” said Mullah, “the cat must have had a visit from a tom cat! Between them they will have eaten the meat.”

“Come to think of it, there was a tom cat in the house yesterday!” said Fatimah.

"How could a cat weighing 2 kg, have eaten 4 kg meat?" said Mullah.

Mullah Nasr al-Din and the Joshing Youths

It was a beautiful sunny day in early spring; the sun was shining and a gentle wind was blowing life into all living animals and plants.

Mullah Nasr al-Din was up at dawn, saying his prayers and thanking God for his fortune. He was full of the joys of spring and, after a little breakfast, went to the garden where his donkey had free range, eating anything which was around in the yard.

"Come on Kasim, let's get out and have some fresh air and fun," he said, addressing his donkey.

Kasim, the donkey, certainly seemed able to understand Mullah's language and Mullah always insisted that he could converse with him. In this instance the animal seemed happy to stay put, dipping into his sack of barley straw but, devoted to his master, Kasim followed the order.

On that day, Mullah decided to walk along by the side of his donkey. He walked the short length of his narrow lane before reaching a main street. There, he encountered a group of youths, boys about 12-14 years old. Spotting the Mullah, they started laughing and singing,

"Here comes the Mullah and his donkey." One of the youths shouted, "Which one is the donkey?" He pointed his finger at Mullah, whilst others pointed to the donkey. This went on for a bit of time, until one of the youths called, "Where are you going your highness?" whilst the others responded by shouting, "He's off to get his barley straw!"

Mullah was getting angry but he thought of a trick.

"Look boys, I am going to a shop just round the corner. The shop is giving pots of honey away, free of charge this afternoon." On hearing this, the boys all ran off towards the shop as fast as they could so that they didn't miss the free honey.

At last he was alone. He turned to his donkey and asked, "What do you think of my wonderful idea my little four legged friend?" The donkey was speechless. Mullah suddenly jumped up onto the donkey. Pushing his legs inwards, signalling him to move, "Come on, hurry up Kasim, follow those boys; we don't want to miss the free honey pots do we?"

Mullah Nasr al-Din goes to the City

Mullah Nasr al-Din, had never been out of his little town, other than to Qom; that was way back when he was a student for a short time at the Islamic School in that holy city. Nevertheless, he had his ear to the ground and kept abreast of news from the cities by frequent visits to the coffee houses and small Bazaars in his little town. Furthermore, as a Mullah it was part of his duties to spread the message of Allah wherever the population gathered.

As the Mullah was approaching his 60th birthday, he thought it was time to expand his knowledge, explore the wonders of the modern world and let his beloved donkey see some new pastures. The Now-Ruz – New Year's Day of the Persian Calendar – seemed a good time to get on with the project, given that nothing was likely to happen for the next two weeks after the new year, because most people would celebrate the Now-Ruz for at least a week, then take things easy for another few days.

Mullah carefully planned his itinerary for the visit, passing through one or two cities before reaching the holy city of Qom as his final destination. He wanted to experience something he had always dreamt of, which was to ride on a donkey whilst one of his students ran or walked beside the animal, indicating the role of a Mullah as a teacher with "Talabeh" (Islamic Theology Students). The problem was that his donkey was not familiar with the roads outside his town and definitely not in Qom. Donkeys generally like to walk on familiar roads rather than be directed by their rider.

Mullah planned to take four of his devoted, bright young students to accompany him and to share the experience of city life; it would open their eyes to the wonders of the world.

At the time there was no documentation readily available about what to visit or where to get information about the cities to be visited. But stories about cities were passed on, through the Bazaar, like wildfires in a dry forest. However, each time a news item was passed on from one individual to another, there would be additions or substitutions to the initial message. Sometimes the original message was altered so much as to become unrecognizable from its original version. The result was that, by the time the news had travelled one hundred yards through the Bazaar, it would have become totally distorted.

Mullah had all the information about the cities he planned to visit, the first being Qazvin. For this journey he joined a camel caravan; at the time this was the only mode of regular travel between the villages and towns which was available to an ordinary citizen. However, considering Mullah's affection for his donkey he preferred to tag on to a caravan but ride his donkey, rather than on a camel. On this occasion he borrowed another donkey from a friend, in order to have a spare donkey to carry things of importance and maybe items that he might buy to bring back as souvenirs or presents for friends.

The Caravan consisted of a dozen or more camels connected head to tail by a length of rope. The ropes passed through the nose ring of one camel and was tied to the saddle of the camel in front. Each row of camels was led by an experienced man – the guardian – who would hold the rope in the ring nose of the first camel and lead the row.

Depending on the number of camels be an additional guide and guards in the middle and at the end of the row. One in every 5 or 6 camels had a bell, with its own characteristic tone, which rang with the movement of the camel.

Mullah on his donkey and the students on camels, travelled for two days and nights. The caravan master used the sun during the day and stars at night to lead the caravan, from what seemed like narrow tracks from nowhere to nowhere, to reach Qazvin.

Mullah and his students arrived in the late evening in Qazvin and stayed for the night at a Caravanserai. In the morning it was a beautiful sunny day and Mullah took his students around the city of Qazvin. Not far from the caravanserai, the students saw a couple of tall factory chimneys. They had never seen anything like it before; smoke was pouring from one of the chimneys.

"Look Master, what are these tall things?" they asked Mullah.

"Well," said Mullah, "these are water wells that have been cleaned and put upside down under the sun to dry.

One of the bright students called Ahmad, who had good eyesight said, "Master there is white smoke coming out of one of the wells."

"Of course," replied Mullah. "This is a bit of water vapour coming out, as the well is drying under the sun."

The students were amazed at the master's knowledge. Mullah seemed to have the answer for all things.

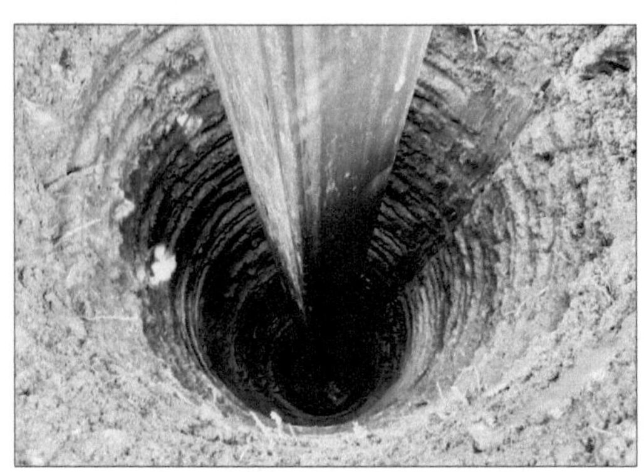

Above: A water well in a village, town or various places in the cities in old Persia to get fresh water

Below: Image of Chimney in town as seen by the Mullah and his students

Mullah Nasr al-Din collecting "Zakat"

One of the most important duties of the Mullah was to go round his parishioners and collect the Zakat, which is a kind of wealth tax incumbent on all Muslims, to help the poor and others according to defined criteria.

Mullah Nasr al Din Mullah did not like being a tax collector, even for Allah, and confessed this to his donkey in no uncertain terms.

Why confess to his donkey, one may ask? Because Mullah's donkey was not an ordinary donkey which was only expected to know the roads that their owners took for work. Mullah's donkey knew the houses in the district, using its ears like satellite navigation; also, it understood the mood of its master. In the case of Zakat, the donkey could sense which individuals did not want to part with their cash with ease.

Mullah had already noticed that when the donkey arrived to the brownish coloured front door of a certain gentleman called Nassir, it would start to bray and kick. Furthermore, it would not stop the hideous noise until someone opened the door.

It is said that, at one occasion when Mullah's donkey arrived at the door of Nassir, it started to bray and kick as usual. When there was no response, it indicted to Mullah to step down so that it could, with its hind legs, kick the door. On this occasion, the donkey nearly broke down the door before at last, a little, fat young woman appeared in the partially open doorway. She was covered head to toe by a black Chador, looking like an overfed crow.

"Salaam alaik Mullah," (greetings) she called. "I cannot ask you in as my husband is praying."

"Where is your husband praying?" asked Mullah.

"He is upstairs, but he has just started and cannot be disturbed, as you appreciate," said the wife.

"It is a strange time for prayer, in the middle of afternoon," said Mullah.

"That is true, but he forgot the midday prayer, so he owed God a prayer; he wanted to pay his dues for the missed prayer," said Nassir's wife.

"He owes a great deal more to his God in Zakat," replied Mullah.

Mullah then decided to leave and come back the next day but he left a message for Nassir not to owe any outstanding prayer for the next day when he was going to return. The next day, at the agreed time, Mullah returned – with the usual reticence of his donkey to turn into Nassir's road. The wife opened the door with some delay.

"I hope your husband is not owing a prayer today. Could you please tell him that I am here to collect the Zakat?"

"I am sorry Mullah, my husband has gone to town for some essential shopping," said the wife.

Mullah jumped back onto his donkey and, as usual facing backwards whilst riding, left the house. As the donkey started to trot away from the house and since he was facing backward, Mullah caught sight of Abu Nassir, peeping through the first floor curtain.

Mullah now returned to the house, he said to Nassir's wife who was still at the door, "Please tell your husband that he should not look through the curtain when he goes shopping!"

Mullah Nasr al-Din, the Sage of Kakin

Kakin is a little village in the province of Qazvin in the northwest of Iran (Persia).

In the olden days in Persia, each village used to have a 'Sage'; a wise man of great experience, wisdom and sensibility to whom complicated family problems or complex issues could be referred for advice and resolution.

He would hold audience and anyone who had problems would attend to present them, and the Sage would solve and advise accordingly. He was also the judge, trying to adjudicate in disputes and matrimonial issues.

A Monshi (a secretary/recorder) would make an official recording of the proceedings for posterity and future reference.

The Sage of the village, in some cases, was ridiculously inadequate – a simpleton and the subject of jokes by villagers. Like many of the villages across the land, Kakin had such a Sage; Mullah Nasr al-Din, generally known as The Mullah. As the name suggests he was a member of clergy but no one knew where he had studied or was ordained.

In Kakin he was adviser to all inhabitants irrespective of their religious belief. He was particularly in demand when there was a dispute or fear of an epidemic or such like. Give him a real difficult problem – he would sort it in no time!! His advice would be executed whatever the consequences might be.

The Mullah would hold audience once a month on a Thursday in Kakin, in a large room, richly carpeted with silk Persian carpets, at one corner of which there was a platform with an ornate chair on which he would sit to deliver his pearls of wisdom. He was never far away from his donkey, which was in a corner of the room quietly dipping into his sack of hay.

Mullah was reputed to sit on his donkey facing backwards and the animal knew where to go, a kind of satnav incorporated donkey! This allowed Mullah to more comfortably look at the landscape backwardly without worrying about the route ahead, which would have been the case if he were seated facing forward.

In the year 1280 of the Persian Calendar (1901 AD), there was an incident in Kakin, the like of which no one had seen or recorded before; this required an urgent resolution; just the kind of thing that was within the domain of the Sage.

A thirsty cow had wondered out of her shed, going to the farmhouse where there was a terracotta pot which usually contained a lot of water. On this occasion, however, there was only a little water, at the bottom of the pot. The cow was trying to drink the water by putting her head right down into the pot. But then the head stuck in the pot and she could not get it out.

Her loudly amplified and echoing "mooing" from within the pot, could be heard a long distance away. People rushed to the farmhouse thinking that an extra-terrestrial had descended from the sky with a message. Alas, there was no extra-terrestrial creature; only the head of a terrestrial cow stuck in the pot, generating the strange noises.

Now, everyone was in a panic and was suggesting ways of getting the head out without breaking the pot, which in Kakin was a vital possession for storage and cooling of water. This was obviously a case for The Sage-Mullah.

Asghar, a 10 year old boy was the fast runner of the village and was asked to run and fetch Mullah for his help, whilst the excited crowd around the distressed cow were trying to hold on to her tail in order to immobilize her and prevent damage to the pot.

"Put on your giveh – don't run barefoot, as there could be snakes on the road," shouted Asghar's mother.

Off went Asghar, running as fast as he could to Mullah's house.

Giveh[7]

After a time, someone standing near the door of the farmhouse shouted: "He is here; I can see the head of a donkey in the dust, it is definitely him." Yes, Mullah was dashing to the scene. Someone ran and helped him off his donkey.

Now there was a complete silence and all eyes focused on the Sage's mouth.

---

[7] *Giveh is a kind of shoe – soft, comfortable, durable and hand woven top with a light leather sole, common in several parts of Iran especially in rural and mountainous areas*

"Well now," said Mullah, "What is all this excitement about? *Have you never seen a cow's head stuck in a pot before?"*

A mischievous looking little boy in the front row shouted, "Yes, but not uncooked!! His mother silenced him by twisting his ear.

"Calm down everyone," said Mullah Nasr al-Din.

"You need to do two things: first, I suggest you sever the cow's head but I want women and children out before you start."

This was done and the head of the cow was duly severed. As expected, the head fell promptly into the bottom of the pot.

"Now", said the Sage, "I want you to break the pot and get the head out."

The deed was done.

Effectively the head of the cow was out of the pot but –gone was the cow and broken was the pot.

The moral of the story:

Think before you take drastic decisions, even if suggested by a Sage!

Note about Kakin

Kakin is a real village and is shown on Wikipedia. The story is a myth.

Kakin was established as a village and was owned by my Grandad.

During the reign of Mohamed Reza Pahlavi my step uncle Mansour Rohani, who was initially the Minister of Agriculture and then the Minister of Energy and Water, was gently persuaded by the Shah to ask my Granddad to donate Kakin to the crown to be distributed between farmers. For my Granddad it was a pleasure to comply!! And it was done. Supposedly, the vast farm should have been divided between small farmers. I, with my family, were living in Geneva at the time and I cannot verify as to whether the land was ever distributed to the small farmers or was annexed to the wealth of the Shah. In any case, under Islamic rules my mother being a woman and a Baha'i, would not have had any claim to part inheritance of it, particularly after the revolution by Khomeini.

I visited Kakin during a school holiday with my older brother and have documented my adventures there under my memory of my school days.

I have obviously put a great touch of me into this story!

A Persian water storage pot

The Rooster of Frahang Avenue

In the 1880s, Farhang Avenue was a middle class, residential area of Tehran, where many of the inhabitants had their own houses and worked as civil servants, shopkeepers or middle ranking army officers. Most of the houses in the street had orchards and vegetable gardens. Characteristically, many residents would grow vegetables and fruit for their own consumption. Some had chickens for food and eggs, a goat or two for milk and a donkey for transport and for carrying bulk shopping, which was the normal way of buying food in bulk, for most of the families living in that population. Amongst the poultry, some house owners kept a couple of cockerels whose function was to make sure that eggs were fertilized for the continuation of the chicken population and, importantly, to announce the sunrise and herald the time to start daily chores – not forgetting prayer.

The houses were separated by tall walls made of mud bricks, so that neighbours could not gaze into the garden or buildings of adjacent houses.

Ali and Reza lived at number 3 and number 5 Farhang Avenue; they were friends working different shifts in Shahre-Dari – the city council.

As neighbours, they used to help one another and they made a passage through a large arch, with a gate between their respective gardens, so that their children could play together and they, themselves, could go and have a smoke of ghalyoon (Hubble Bubble) and enjoy tea in one another's houses, particularly during Fridays when they were off work.

In those days, tea was always available in Persian homes, from early morning to late at night, because the Samavar, that great tea making device, would be well stocked with charcoal with the tea pot on the top of its chimney, providing ever hot tea.

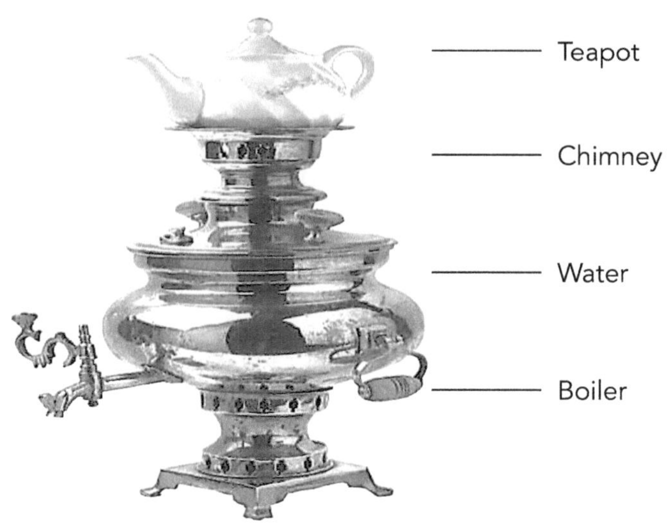

The Samovar / Samavar

The *Samovar/Samavar is a metal water container, traditionally used to heat and boil water for making tea with a designated lodge to place a teapot. It consists of a large metal container with a tap near the bottom and a metal pipe running vertically through the middle. Its components are:*

1) *A boiler which is a water container of different capacity with a tap at the bottom for delivering hot water to make tea.*
2) *Fuel container that in the olden days used charcoal for heating, basically providing heat energy when ignited.*

3) *A chimney which is a tube leading from the fuel container, the top of which has a place which accommodate the tea pot.*
4) *the heater and chimney are surrounded by a "belly", the boiler which is the water reservoir.*
5) *At the top of the chimney there is a place for the teapot.*
6) *This tea making machine (device) boils water which makes concentrated tea that in turn can be kept warm at all times and be diluted with water from the boiler to the required strength.*

For a number of years Ali and Reza and their respective families lived in harmony and enjoyed a friendly relationship. But, with the arrival of a new rooster within Ali's population of birds, all this changed. The problem arose as a result of the disorderly behaviour of Ali's new cockerel. To understand how, one has to appreciate the unwritten rule which was operational between the birds of Farhang Avenue.

Ali possessed 14 chickens and 2 roosters. Reza had only 8 chickens and 1 cockerel. It was the young rooster of Ali, recently added to the troupe which succeeded to disturb the peace.

The rooster was called Rostam, named after the legendary and mythical Persian warrior hero. This rooster had an unusual comb and a set of magnificent wattles to go with it, which could attract any hen within the 22 female birds of Ali and Reza put together. If that wasn't enough to cause trouble, Rostam had the loudest, the longest and the most ear piercing 'Ghoo-ghoolo-Ghoo-Ghool' crow. These attributes drove him to a few fights with the two older cock birds called Shirr (Lion) and Pallang (Tiger) respectively. These skirmishes resulted in him establishing his superiority in the eyes of the hen population of both houses. But what nearly cost Rostam his head was that he tried to out-do the other cockerels, not only of Numbers 3 and 5 but also the other roosters within almost a kilometre of Ali's house.

In Farhang Avenue at the time, ordinary people would wake and rise with the crowing of cockerels; this announced sunrise and time to pray before going to work.

Prior to the arrival of Rostam, Shir used to be the first cock to herald the dawn with his crowing. After a while, Pallang would respond to Shir, presenting his homage to Shir as 'cock of the walk'.

When the new, unruly Rostam arrived it would start crowing before the others, usually before sunrise. Reza was disturbed by being waken up in the middle of the night by this stupid bird. He discussed this with Ali, its owner, who could only laugh.

One night, Reza 'flipped'. Nights of insomnia culminated; he would take drastic action. As Rostam was sitting in a prominent place, crowing at the top of his voice and proudly showing off his wattles, with extended neck, Reza threw a blanket over him and captured the bird.

In no time, Rostam was under Reza's left arm, whilst his right hand was trying to wring his neck. The rooster was struggling for its life, crowing for all he was worth. He was not going to die without a fight.

By this time Ali had been woken up with all the noise; he rushed to the scene.

"What on earth are you doing, Reza?" screamed Ali. "I'm winding up the clock, Ali," responded Reza, letting go of the bird. Rostam's head was saved in the nick of time.

Reza is wringing the neck of the rooster, saying
"I am winding the clock"

The fright the bird had received certainly changed him for the better; he continued to be the top rooster but it was said that his crowing was now more 'pianissimo' and he was friendlier towards the other older roosters, Shir and Pallang.

More importantly, he started crowing at a later time in the morning, since the other cockerels accepted him as the top rooster. He also continued to be the Don Giovani of the chicken world!

Appendix

A Religious Calling

Archaeological evidence reveals an abundance of domestic fowl in the Middle Ages. For a sustainable community, the breeding of chickens would have been a must, which would have required roosters – who appeared to have a prominent role in calling practitioners to pre-dawn devotions. In the 6th century, cockcrow constituted one of the four periods of night time devotion for monasteries that followed the precepts maintained by the Rule of the Master (Regula Magistri). This required psalms be said at nightfall, midnight, cockcrow and in the morning. The period denoted by the rooster's crow helped manage devotions in the face of seasonal changes: psalms were said prior to the cockcrow in the winter, and after the cockcrow in the summer to account for the shifting durations of darkness. Roosters, with their noisy pronouncements, also alerted those living beyond the immediate reach of religious orders to ready themselves for morning devotions.

The connection between the rooster and the coming dawn offered fertile ground for associations with light and spirituality.

Source: *Varia*

The Shopkeeper and his Parrot

In the 1930s, Tehran, the capital city of what was Persia – now Iran – was a complex city with a definite North-South divide. The north of Tehran was affluent with large houses and modern buildings, spacious avenues and boulevards, modern shops and stores of all kinds; one could, at the time, find a variety of Persian and foreign wines and spirits on sale openly, as well as meat and sausages of pork provenance.

In the south of the city, streets were narrow, some were only covered with cobblestone or gravel and others were just dirt tracks.

Most of the streets in the south of Tehran, in the 1930s, were dark at night, without proper lighting. Shops were confined to general stores selling all sorts of groceries; anything from candles to rice and charcoal to a variety of spices. Meat and bread had their own shops. Many types of bread were made freshly whilst the customers queued and waited their turn.

Amongst many other things, these stores served as a meeting place for the shoppers, who would gather to chat and spread news or gossips and have a glass of tea which was prepared in a Samovar and served in small glasses or *Stekan*. Most customers knew the shopkeepers or were related to them; they would come to buy some items, then stay to chat and sometimes have a smoke of ghalyoon, with their glass of tea.

Quite a few of these shops had a cat or two, which were functional in keeping the mice from the foodstuff; they may also have a bird of paradise, which was more ornamental.

My grandmother was a great babysitter for a number of her grandchildren, some of whom lived next door to her; she was always in demand.

We, the children, used to gather with considerable excitement in our grandmother's house, showing our excitement with the usual children's noise. However, as soon as she started with the equivalent of, 'Once upon a time,' all would fall silent.

She knew and would recount many stories related to birds and animals.

One of these was concerned with a specially gifted parrot which was owned by Hassan, who had a corner shop in one of the affluent areas near the centre of Tehran. Hassan loved his parrot and did not keep it in cage. However, at the entrance to his shop, there was a curtain made of strings of beads, which were fashionable at the time.

The problem with Hadji, the parrot, was that he was too talkative, even when there were customers in the shop. Not only was Hadji talkative but he would repeat some of the sales patter used by his master to his customers. This would be followed by bird laughter. Although Hassan loved Hadji, he used to punish him several times a day for his cheek, by hitting the bird on the top of the head. After a time, Hadji lost his feathers on the top of his head and remained silent. He became depressed and introvert.

Hassan was extremely worried and sad. He tried hard to get a word out of his previously lovable and chatty companion. This went on for some time, until the day a customer came into the shop who was wearing neither a hat nor a turban, which were worn at the time by all men. The man who entered the shop was bald.

Now, for the first time after a long period Hadji opened his beak to speak:

"What wrong words have you spoken to have become bald?" he squawked.

The poor bird clearly thought that, in this man, he had found a kindred spirit who had also been subjected to cruel behaviour. His master hung his head in shame.

Hadji asking the bald man what wrong words he has spoken to end up being bald.

Smart Parrot

There are many long-held traditions in Persian culture which have been passed on from generation to generation and have been kept alive or even translated into foreign languages by Iranian ex-patriots, for the benefit of their descendants who may never see the country of origin of their parents or grandparents. One such tradition concerns those who go away from home to distant lands for business or study; they are expected to bring back to family and close friends, a souvenir of what they have tasted or seen in foreign lands

Solayman was a respectable merchant who lived in the city of Kernam in south east of Persia. He traded in spices, rice and a variety of exotic beans, peas and lentils, mostly imported from China and India.

Solayman's family consisted of three people and a bird. His wife, Leyla, was a typical wife and a mother, taking care of everything at home and being an accomplished cook. His daughter, Yasmin, was a designer of the famous Kerman 'Laver Tree' silk carpets in a carpet factory in the city. The third member of the family was a teenage girl, Zobaydeh, who was a servant; traditionally these young servants were treated as a member of the family and were counted as such. The bird of the family was Baback, a speaking parrot. Baback was housed in an ornate cage with many mirrors, real small trees and a tropical jungle-like environment.

In the year 1206 Solayman was about to undertake a long journey from Kerman to various parts of India. The whole journey would take about 3 months. Before the start of the journey he gathered his family around, asking them what they would like him to bring back for them. His wife wanted a dress made of Batik, his daughter, then 9 years old, asked to have a mirror in a nice Indian frame and Zobaydeh asked for a brass candle stick.

This family gathering took place in the presence of Baback the parrot, stuck in his cage. Seeing that he was being missed from the list and passed over, without being asked what he wanted, he started to shout: "What about Baback? What about Baback?"

"What about Baback?" asked the parrot

Solayman turned to the parrot. "What would my beloved bird want me to bring him from India; a pretty female bird companion, maybe?"

"Master I don't want anything, but maybe you will pass on a message of friendship from me when you see a lonely parrot flying," replied Baback.

"What do you want me to tell him?" asked Solayman.

"Tell him that you have a parrot, called Baback, who has a fantastic cage with a high roof allowing him to expand his wings," replied Baback.

"Anything else?" asked Solayman.

"Yes Master," answered Baback. "If you happen to go to a forest you will see many parrots sitting in trees conversing and joking with their little ones. Please give them my greetings and tell them that I'd like to visit them one day."

A few days later, camels and donkeys were gathered in a Caravanserai outside the gate of Kerman, ready to start the journey. Food and merchandise, especially carpets, were loaded onto animals and guides and guards were hired for the journey. Crowds of family, friends and townsfolk gathered at the gate of the city to say farewell to Solayman, and his fellow travellers. Out through the gate of the city they went and began their journey.

Barely a day into the journey, Solayman was sitting comfortably between the two humps of a camel, when he saw a single parrot circling high over the caravan; he seemed to be showing the direction to a nearby caravanserai.

Solayman invited the parrot to sit upon the front hump of his camel so that he could pass on his own parrot's message. Warily, the wild parrot accepted the invitation and Solayman then repeated, almost word by word, the message that Baback had given him.

"You see," said Solayman, "I have a parrot called Baback, who has a beautiful cage, with a high roof, which is big enough for him to expand his wings. When I asked him what he wanted me to bring back for him from India, he said he didn't want anything; he asked me instead to deliver this message of greetings when I saw a lone parrot, which I now have done."

As soon as Solayman finished the message, the parrot fell motionless to the ground, apparently dead. Solayman was upset by this but needed to continue with his journey.

After a few days of business, he hired some local guides, with the purpose of trying to forget the dead bird. He went into the forest where parrots were supposed to congregate. After a long walk and hard work to clear the way, notwithstanding mosquito bites and the many dangerous looking insects, at last he saw a group of parrots on a branch of a tree.

"Hello friends," he shouted. "I have come from a faraway land to bring you a goodwill message from my dear parrot, Baback."

The very mention of the name Baback provoked a salvo of repetitious, "Baback, Baback, Baback" from the birds and then kind of laugh.

"Hear me please," pleaded Solayman. There was, at last, quiet. Solayman continued, "I would like to tell you about my parrot Baback; he wishes me to tell you that he would like to visit you one day, to tell you about his adventures if he can. Have you got any message from him that I can take back?"

Disaster then struck. As soon as he had delivered the message, a number of birds fell from the tree and died.

"Oh my goodness, what is going on here?" sighed Solayman.

He and his guides were shocked; they returned tearfully to the city.

As soon as Solayman delivered the message of his parrot, Baback, many of the parrots on the tree fell seemingly dead.

The rest of his time in India was spent in buying the presents for his wife and other members of his family.

The time came to round up the caravan and prepare the merchandise to be loaded on the animals ready to move on.

After a couple of weeks of travel, they could see the top of the Jameh Mosque, indicating that they were now near Kerman and soon would see their family.

Solayman was worried about not having anything for Baback; there was only the mystery of the parrots' death. How could he tell Baback that there was no message from them? He decided, at first, to say that he was unable to see the parrots but he couldn't face to lie to his dear parrot and decided to pray for a solution. At last he entered the gate of the city and went straight home. Everyone welcomed him and he distributed the presents to all.

In the joy and curiosity of finding out who got what, everyone asking Solayman about what he had seen in his travels, Baback's voice was ear piercing, repeatedly shouting, "What about me? What about me? What about me?"

"Yes, what about him?" asked Yasmin.

Solayman paused and, for a minute, he was silent with a sad expression; all eyes in the room were fixed on him. He approached Baback's cage and became tongue tied.

"Did you encounter any parrots, Master?" asked Baback.

"Not only did I but I made a point of going to the Forest as you had asked me to do," replied Solayman.

Baback asked "Did you give them my message, Master?"

"Indeed I did," replied Solayman.

"Did they give you any message to bring back for me?"

"No, they did not," replied Solayman

"What happened then?"

"I don't know how to tell you. As soon as I delivered your message they fell and died. I wasn't going to tell you but here is an unfortunate truth. That is what happened. None of the parrots gave any message," replied Solayman, who could not look straight at Baback.

Hearing this, Baback had a seizure and fell motionless in his cage. This was, of course, what Solayman was really afraid might happen. Great sadness replaced the homecoming joy for all.

"Father, why has Baback died?" Asked Yasmin.

"I have no idea," answered Solayman. "Maybe because of the shock of hearing that the other parrots in India died because of the message he had sent."

The whole family wept for Baback.

However, Solayman as the head of the family wiped his tearful eyes and said, "This is God's will and we must accept it and be grateful that it was not one of us." Then, opening the door of the cage, as a sign of respect for Baback, he placed the limp body of the bird on a wide branch of a tree.

As the whole family stood silently around the tree in quiet respect, there was a little movement of the head of Baback. The family watched in awe as, a few minutes later, Baback woke up and flew away to sit on the wall of the house.

"Thank you, Master, for delivering my message to my friends in India and for bringing their message back to me."

The message they sent was to tell me how to become a free bird; I love you all very dearly, but I would rather be free in the forest with all its dangers than to live in luxury in a cage. Forgive me Master! Please come to see me in India."

As the bird flew away, Solayman shouted: "My dear Baback, we love you too, we would rather see you happy living away from us than unhappy living with us.

"Good luck and farewell, you can always come back, the door of your cage will be open for ever and will remain open for you to come and go as you wish."

Leyla then narrated a short couplet by an amateur Persian female poet; Azizeh Rohani: "Fly away my beloved, with God as your companion. May my prayer protect you in your time of need."

Sam goes to Tehran

Sam (Samuel) had travelled nearly five days from Qazvin to get to Tehran; he was going to live with his uncle Mousa. At last the gate of the city of Tehran was within sight. The journey had been lonely and, had it not been because of the unexpected death of his father, he could not have endured to be away from his widowed mother. He had just turned 16 – a couple of weeks since – when his father passed away with a sudden massive heart attack.

During the journey, his companion was his donkey, Souski – Sousk is a black beetle in Farsi. Souski was, indeed, a female black donkey; a loyal animal who never left the sight of Sam. She would not eat or drink when Sam stopped for a rest without first seeing the boy taking water and food.

Sam had all his possession packed in two bags on the back of Souski; the donkey was clad with a nice carpet and a saddle for Sam to sit on. The animal would walk and even run with all the belongings of her master on her back though, much of the time, the donkey had to carry Sam as well, who would sit on the saddle in front of the bags.

Now, not far from his destination, it was the moment for rest and reflection before entering the gate of this new life that had been forced upon him because of the death of his father.

He decided to camp for the night, leaving his donkey as a 'guard' outside the tent to watch for the hungry wolves which usually scavenged near to city gates at night.

When Sam's father died, by tradition Sam's uncle became the head of the family and responsible for taking charge of the well-being of the wife of his brother, as well as overseeing the education or apprenticeship of the children.

Although Sam and his family were Jewish, they were not strict in the practice of Judaism; they followed the unwritten laws of family life which had long been established in Persia.

Sam's uncle, Mousa had a shop in Bazaar-eh-Shah, (the king's Bazaar) of Tehran, trading in Qazvin's specialty, velvet; he was expert on trading in these specific items. The idea of asking his nephew to come to Tehran, was to teach the boy what he knew about textiles and, above all, how to trade in textiles. Mousa did not have a son and, again according to tradition, Sam was destined to become part of the business of his uncle. Like many of the teenagers from the countryside, Sam had a bit of a disadvantage compared with boys of his age who had been born and brought up in Tehran. He knew that he must try to learn to speak Farsi with the accent of the Tehran inhabitants, to send the message to other traders that he was not naïve and had experience in handling both traders and customers.

Given the fact that his uncle had only one daughter, all eyes in the family were focused on Sam to become the person who would learn the tricks of the trade and prepare himself to join the business of his uncle. Also, business aside, even when his father was alive, Sam was the first choice to be married to his cousin, Macha, the 15 years old daughter of his uncle. For some time before the death of his father, Sam's mother Tahila and his uncle's wife Esther had plans that one day Sam and Macha would marry, thus keeping the family together.

Now here, not far from the gate of Tehran, Sam decided to camp for the night near the edge of a small river, as he was advised to do by his uncle. He remembered two specific pieces of advice, given by his uncle, before the start of his journey. First, that he must realize that there are many thieves in a big city; they looked and talked like a friend, with the ulterior motive of finding out if the stranger was carrying any money, gold or silver with him. Sam should be wary of those who present themselves as a friend, who in reality are 'a wolf in sheep's clothing.'

Also, in the city centre in particular, which was a very crowded place, some thieves worked as a gang. Like a pack of wolves, one member of the gang draws your attention away from your belongings, another one or two then steal your possessions.

"Don't let go of the reins of your donkey for a second," had advised the uncle," because they have a way of silently taking away an animal."

These thieves would gather a few animals, similar to that of the stranger who was coming to town and congregate in a crowded place, such as near the Bazaar, in order to confuse the stranger into thinking that someone had the same donkey as his. This provided a distraction which allowed the thieves to take the reins out of the hand of the owner. The animal would then be taken away into the crowd, mingling with the gang members with the similar looking donkey. When the owner approached the person leading the animal, thinking that it was his own, he soon found out that it was not; his own donkey and belongings were far away.

So, Sam was advised to spend the night outside the city so that, "You and your mind are sharp when you enter the city."

Sam did precisely that. He put up his tent and, for the first time, he lit his candle and started to pray, thanking God for helping him to reach safely close to his destination. He went into deep thought. He was almost ashamed that he, at his age, was truly missing his mother. He vowed to bring his mother to Tehran as soon as he possibly could. The final melancholic thought of the night, before putting out his light, was a couplet poem written and given to him by his grandmother, with the instruction that he should read it just before entering the city of Tehran. It read:

'Now go on with your journey my dear heart, with God by your side, and my prayer will be your protector and your guide.'

Sam's night was sleepless. After five days and nights on the road, with the thought of what might lie ahead, any man would stay awake, let alone a teenager.

Early in the morning Sam started the penultimate part of his journey towards one of the gates of Tehran known as the "Gate of Qazvin". As he was reaching the threshold of the Gate he noticed more and more travellers converging from all directions.

It was clear to him that his chances of getting to the Bazaar during daylight, to meet his uncle, were remote. As he was toiling with the idea of how best to proceed, he met a man called Hajji Ali-Reza, who said he was going to the mosque which was situated inside the gate. Clearly, he was religious and showed great understanding of the plight of a 16 year country boy coming to the big city.

Hajji Ali thought that the idea of leaving the donkey in the stable of the mosque for a few hours was an obvious solution to Sam's problems of not knowing how to get to Bazaar and risking losing his donkey.

Sam reached the mosque and asked if he could leave his donkey there for a few hours. Unfortunately, he found that the mosque only had sufficient space for the worshipers who attended the mosque for prayer. This meant that he would have to go in to pray as if he were a Moslem and, if it was discovered that he was a Jew, the least that could happen was that he would be beaten for having entered the Mosque and his donkey would be taken away from him.

He wondered if the Hajji Ali Reza would be able to take his donkey and keep it in the Mosque for him for a few hours, so he timidly and respectfully asked the Hajji if he would could consider the proposal. “My dear young man you are not in Qazvin where you can ask this kind of service from a busy person like me. No, I have no time for that,” said Hajji Ali.

“I am sorry sir, I did not mean to offend you. I am willing to pay the small amount money that I can afford,” said Sam. Since the answer was still negative, they parted and Sam decided to rely on his own initiative and find his way to the Bazaar. He started to walk, leading his donkey and looking at the rough route map given to him by his uncle.

Whilst he was walking away from the gate, it suddenly occurred to him that it was lucky that he had not left his donkey with Hajji. This was exactly what he had been told not to do by his uncle inside or around the city wall of Tehran. He clearly remembered being told about those ‘wolves clad in sheep’s clothing’. Suddenly, he heard someone shouting his name; “Sam! Sam stop!”

Sam stopped and looked back; Hajji Ali was calling him. He appeared to have had second thoughts about not keeping the donkey. That second thought was a temptation.

“I should have taken the donkey and all the Sam’s belongings – not temporarily, but permanently!” he said to himself. His sin would be mitigated as Sam was a Yahoodie or Jew; robbing him would be of little consequence! It was with this in mind that he ran after Sam and called him to stop. He reached Sam and put his arm on the shoulder of the boy.

"I am sorry to have acted badly towards you and not have heeded your request. I have had second thoughts and would like to say that I am willing to hold your donkey in the Mosque's stable and you need not to pay anything," he said. He extended his hand to take the leather rope of the harness of the donkey. But Sam was now alert.

"I, also, have had second thoughts and my donkey and I have decided that we would rather find our own way to the Bazaar. We thank you nevertheless for your noble gesture towards us, the strangers."

Sam continued to walk, squeezing the ring that his Grandmother had put on his ring finger at the start of his journey, to remind his to be wary of evil people. He whispered to himself, "I thank you Grandma, you promised that God would be with me."

As he walked, looking again at the letter and the drawing given to him by his uncle as a guide to get to the Bazaar, he suddenly noticed that, on its margin, there was some writing underlined, which read, 'In case of difficulty, go to the Coffee House which is on the straight cobblestone road near the Gate of Qazvin, called 'Dawood Coffee House'. The owner's name is Jamshid who is a relative of your Aunt Fareeda; ask for help.' This was God sent.

"Thank you, Grandma," he murmured to himself. In fact, he was just in front of that very Coffee House. Jamshid was delighted to meet Sam and asked him to stay and have a meal.

In the meantime, he sent a messenger to the Bazaar to inform Sam's uncle of his arrival.

After a couple of hours, Mousa was in the Coffee House. He warmly greeted his nephew and took him to his house. Sam started work in his uncle's shop the next day.

Within a short while he became a proficient salesman and became well known in the part of the Bazaar concerned with textiles.

He eventually developed knowledge in the carpet industry and although Qazvin carpets were not considered as the very top quality, he succeeded to introduce a new design which made them competitive with those of Kashan and Kirman. In no time 'Sam's Carpets' became a shop within the Corridor of the Carpets in the Bazaar. He expanded his uncle's business and became a partner.

Next he brought his mother to Tehran and built a house for them. At the age of 25, barely 9 years after his arrival in Tehran, he was considered wealthy and it was now time to marry his cousin Macha. This was what his father used to talk about and what he aimed for his son.

Sam, sadly, never saw grandmother again; she died a few months after he left Qazvin and he could not go to her funeral. However, he always cherished her memory and kept safe the ring she had given him when he was journeying to Tehran.

The textile and carpet business of the partnership and the family, continued in business and thrived ever after.

Moral: hard work will be rewarded but be wary of the wolf in lamb's clothing!

Suleiman, a Horseshoe and Reza

Suleiman was 40 years old – a fisherman from Rasht.[8] He had a boat and old-fashioned types of fishing nets which he had used since his youth. His fishing gear wasn't as good as many of his contemporaries but he had the knack of finding himself at the right time in the right patch of the water where there were masses of the Caspian Kutum – Caspian white fish – a type suitable to be smoked for making a popular smoked dish, one of the most favourite in Persian cuisine.

He was brought up in a deprived area of the city of Rasht. Almost from birth he knew a boy called Reza, whose mother and his were great friends. Suleiman and Reza went to school together and they both became fishermen. As young men they lived as neighbours in the same street and almost every day after work they went to a coffee shop run by Parviz. They would sit in the same place, which was reserved for them. At dawn they would go down together to their own individual boats.

The life of fishermen has always been hard, requiring patience, good health, experience and luck to achieve a good catch. Suleiman appeared to enjoy the challenge of it all.

One day, when pulling in his net, Suleiman found an unusual thing in his catch which, after closer inspection, turned out to be a horseshoe. This was a good omen and he cleaned and polished it and became obsessed with thinking that it was God sent.

He took his find to a blacksmith he knew, to find out more

---

8 Rasht is the largest city on Iran's Caspian Sea coast.

about it. Close examination by Issa, his friend, proved this horseshoe to be an old one which had been used by a small foal. Issa advised him that, for good luck, he should nail the horseshoe to the mast of his boat.

However, Suleiman had a better idea; he would expand his business. Instead of selling his catch to restaurants and fish merchants, which he had done for years, he would deliver the fish direct to the customers and become a street fish seller.

He bought himself a small cart, painted it in dark red and blue and printed his name "Suleiman the Fish Merchant" on each side of the cart. Next, he went around the stables he knew of to buy a foal. Not just any foal – one with three shoes.

That proved a mammoth task and eventually he agreed on a compromise: he would buy a foal and ask for one of its shoes to be removed and use in its place the one that he had found.

He now had a business; he was not just a fisherman but also a fish trader with a boat, a cart and a horse, albeit a little one. He worked practically day and night and was amassing a fair amount of money; so much as to allow him to buy a bigger house in a more affluent part of Rasht.

However, whereas when he was a fisherman he had plenty of time to spend with his friends in coffee shops and was engaged to be married to a sister of his friend, he was now gradually losing his friends. He had become a stranger to his pals and those with whom he had been to school. More importantly, he was not seeing Reza; too busy, too occupied with business, he was becoming a kind of robot. He came to be referred to by old friends and acquaintances as Suleiman Khan and not simply Suleiman.

A couple of years passed and one day he went to the coffee shop that he used to go into. The owner, Parviz, came and greeted him as Suleiman Khan and asked him where he would like to sit and would he like to have a smoke of ghalyoon – hubble-bubble – in a more private place.

He told Parviz, "I am not Suleiman Khan, I am Suleiman and want to sit in my usual place with my old friend Reza who used to come in here about this time every day."

"Alas, Suleiman Khan, Reza does not come here since his eight year old boy died six months ago."

"Why did no one tell me?" asked Suleiman.

"Well, you are not one of us anymore; you moved away and old friends did not want to bother you," came the answer.

"Where can I find him? Does he still live around Nassir Shah Street?" asked Suleiman.

"No," answered Parviz, "Unfortunately he got into serious debt and he is now a beggar; he sleeps on the street near Imam Hossein Mosque."

Suleiman said nothing further. He left the coffee shop and went straight to the Mosque of Imam Hossein.

Once inside the Mosque he prayed, then he searched outside the Mosque. Eventually he found his childhood friend – dirty, emaciated and hardly awake.

He sat down beside the unshaven, unclean Reza. What happened next was told for many years amongst the fishermen.

Suleiman took Reza to his home. Over the next few weeks he sold his house and bought a house in the district where he once had lived. He also sold his cart and foal, removing the horseshoe from the foal. Lastly, he bought a fishing boat for

Reza and, one morning at dawn, he returned with Reza to fish in the sea – just like the old days.

He took the horseshoe that he had found in his net a couple of years before and threw it out into the sea, looking at the sky and shouting, "Thank you God, for teaching me a lesson in humility. I would rather be as I was, within the community of my friends, instead of being a rich man living without friends."

Reza was not far away and, in turn, thanked God for blessing him with such a good friend.

Municipality of Rasht

The Gambler

Hassan was born into a middle class family in the city of Bushehr, some 1000 miles south of Tehran the capital of Iran. As a boy, he worked as a fisherman near the Persian Gulf. One day, at the age of 14 he had caught a dangerous fish, a shark, which jumped out of his net and bit off one of Hassan's testicles. After several operations he was fortunate to have one functioning testicle.

He excelled at school and after completing his education, succeeded to secure a post in a secretariat of the Ministry of Commerce. He never contemplated getting married, despite his good looks, reasonable income and pressure by his mother to have a wife and children.

He had one major problem, he was a gambling addict. He had once won a fair amount of money but usually he lost on every wager he laid. He lost all his savings, he sold all his possessions but for a bare minimum, yet he could not stop betting on anything which he thought could win him a few Dinars. In desperation, thinking that he must have been cursed, he went to visit a fortune teller and curse remover who had a stall in the Bazaar.

"In your case, I shall remove the curse of your losing and you can test it by one more bet." Hassan believed that he now had the chance to win back his lost fortune.

He thought of an extraordinarily clever bet that he felt he was certain to win. The bet was unusual and he had to find a wealthy gambler with a reputation of taking risks and one known to never turn down a bet.

The bet was a simple one; since only he had the knowledge

of his genital anatomy, he would lay a wager with a normal man that, between two of them they would have 3 testicles and not 4 which would normally be the case for two men.

Nevertheless, he now needed to find the right person who would agree to such a wager.

On advice from the fortune teller and curse remover, he needed to discretely approach a wealthy gambler in the Bazaar who would never refuse a wager, however, big or small. He had to be discrete since, if caught, he would be punished by lashing; the number of lashes matched the importance of the bet.

Ali Akbar Khan (Ali) was a rich pawn broker who also had a carpet shop in Bazaar-e-Shah, the biggest Bazaar in Tehran. He had a reputation for never turning down any bet. He was known both for his wealth and his passion for gambling – *Ghomar Bazi*. He also was famous for his discretion, in equal measure to his wealth. He was exactly the right kind of a man; he fitted the description and characteristics given by the fortune teller.

Hassan went to the shop and after the usual 'Salam -Alayke' greeting, made it clear that he had not come to buy a carpet but wondered whether Akbar Khan was interested in a 'business venture'; the code to discuss a wager.

"Of course, my friend; come and sit and smoke a ghalyoon (Hubble Bubble) and have Chai (tea). There is a private room behind the beaded curtain in the shop." Akbar Khan left a small board, placed on the outside of his shop, which read 'Dear Customer, I am absent temporarily. Please return later.'

Hassan and Akbar Khan retired to the back of the shop; it was lavishly carpeted and had a samovar with ready-made tea in a teapot on its top and a ghalyoon ready to be smoked.

"What is the bet you want to place?" said Akbar Khan.

Hassan said, "It is a difficult and unusual bet and I can quite understand if you feel you don't want to go for it.

"Spell it out Hassan," said Ali Akbar Khan. "Nothing is difficult to say except lies".

"All right, here it is," said Hassan.

"I bet that, between the two of us, we have three testicles and not four," said Hassan.

"What kind of wager is this, my friend?" asked Akbar Khan and added: "Are you sure you want to place a bet on this?"

"Yes very sure," said Hassan, reminding Ali that he had a reputation that he never turned down any bet.

Ali-Akbar Khan tried to persuade Hassan not to place a big bet on this, but Hassan was insistent.

"What kind of money do you want to lay for this wager?" asked Akbar Khan.

"Well, as a matter of fact I have no money but I have a house that maybe you will accept as a pawn to provide the cash for this wager," replied Hassan.

"Alright, my friend. To be honest, your house is not worth much and when it comes to its value as a pawn, it will be of even less value. I will be prepared to give you 1250 Tooman if you win," said Akbar Khan.

"Can we go a bit higher, say 1300 Toomans."

"Alright, so be it," said Akbar.

Akbar Khan now got out his book, in which he duly registered the bet and asked Hassan to put his name; his index finger was placed on an ink pad and its mark made in the book.

Akbar Khan handed over the 1300 Tooman to Hassan who in exchanged signed off his house to Akbar Khan. All done.

Hassan was convinced that he would win the wager and have his house back, together with the 1300 Tooman.

The time came to compare and count testicles. As agreed, on the count of three, both dropped their shalvar and exposed their body for inspection.

Hassan's shock knew no bounds when, on inspection, it became clear that Akbar Khan also had one testicle.

What Hassan did not know was that, several years previously, Akbar Khan was caught gambling by the secret police and had 40 lashes on his backside. Unfortunately, some of the lashes caught his genitals and he lost one of his testicles due to trauma and bleeding. On closer inspection and verification, Hassan realized that he had now lost his house to his gambling.

Yes, yet again Hassan had lost his bet. He now had no money, no belongings and no home. Had it not been for the generosity of Akbar he would have had nowhere to live and no money for his keep. In fact, Akbar Khan decided to give back to Hassan the house he had taken as a pawn; he offered Hassan work as an assistant in his carpet shop – on the condition that he never gambled again.

Hassan kept his word not to ever gamble and worked hard to expand the business of Akbar Khan.

Within a few years he became a partner in the business and started exporting carpets to China, India and Europe. With his experience in the Ministry of Commerce, he became special adviser to the Ministry.

At the age of 38 he married the 25 year old daughter of Akbar Khan, and they all lived happily ever after. And yes, they had 4 children.

The Tailor in the Pot

Once upon a time Kazim, a tailor, had a little shop just inside one of Tehran's gates. Tehran, the capital city of Persia since the Qajar dynasty in 1796, had several gates – 6 or 7 in number.

The Gate of Qazvin in Tehran Circa 1935

The gates had keepers and guardians who were responsible to see that they were closed at sunset and opened at sunrise. They were also watchful of what and who was getting into and out of the city.

Kazim had an obsession with death and was interested to know the number of people who died in the city each day, by recording the number of bodies which were transported, usually by horse and cart, through the gate to the cemetery outside the city.

Although he was quite agile in the use of an abacus in his business, he used a different instrument for calculating the number of dead bodies. He had a simple method, which was to keep a large terracotta pot inside his shop – the type of pot which was commonly in use to store fresh water.

Each time a body was carried through the gate he dropped a stone into the pot.

At the end of a day, or a week, he would empty the pot, count the number of stones and pray for the people whom they represented.

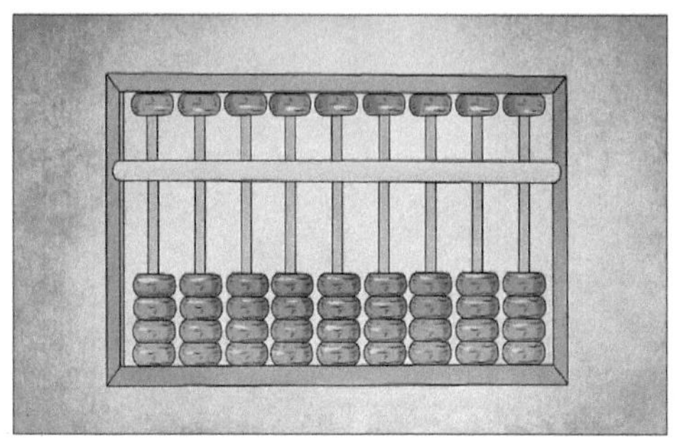

Abacus – An old-fashioned calculator

Persian Terracotta pots for water storage in everyday use.

Kazim watching through the window as a body is carried through the gates and he drops a stone for each one into the pot.

Years went by and, unfortunately, Kazim became ill and shortly afterwards died. Originally, Kazim was from a city called Qazvin, where his brother and family still lived. After his death, one of his friends in Tehran, called Nassir, decided to travel to Qazvin, to break the sad news to his family. He took with him the personal possessions of Kazim, including his terracotta pot; he journeyed in a caravan which consisted of a row of camels which were loosely attached head to tail by a leather cord and travelling in line; they were guided by an old man who knew the unmarked tracks. At night the stars were their guide.

"Caravan"– Rows of Camels often mixed with horses and donkeys for travel

Nassir rode on the first camel, carrying the terracotta pot; he loaded the rest of Kazim's belongings on a few of the other camels in the long line of the caravan.

On arrival to Qazvin, Kazim's nephew was getting married and the family was having a wedding party. Nassir did not quite know how to break the news of Kazim's death; everyone was enjoying the party and asking where Kazim himself was. Nassir felt this was the time for a little oriental subtlety.

Kazim had dropped a stone, representing a body, into a pot whenever a corpse passed through the gate, so, when he died, his friend did the same for him.

When Nassir met the family and was asked for news of the tailor, the friend replied, "He is in the pot," a subtle way of imparting the news that Kazim was dead; for the deceased, being 'in the pot' equated with being dead and was symbolic of the adage that what you do to, or for, others would be done to you in turn.

"What? In the pot?" asked the brother puzzled.

"Yes, in the pot," replied Nassir.

The top of the pot was removed and in it there was a single stone. The brother smiled gently in realization. He knew about the antics of Kazim.

And this story became the origin of the saying: 'The tailor fell in the pot,' implying that someone has fallen victim of the same thing that he or she has been doing as a job or hobby.

Zahhak and Jasmine

Once, far away across the seas and oceans, there was an Empire called Persia, a vast and rich country. Some 3000 years ago, this Empire was ruled by a king named Zahhak; a tyrant, cruel, blood thirsty and evil.

King Zahhak did not like anyone questioning his authority. He would have no hesitation to behead his closest of advisers or ministers if there was a hint of disobedience or disagreement. Like many kings and rulers in those ancient times, Zahhak would have a wife for almost the sole purpose of producing a male child, who would be groomed to become the king, thus securing the succession. Also, like many rulers of the time, he disposed of his queen if the marriage failed to produce a boy and he then moved to the next wife.

Zahhak went through several marriages without any success in producing a prince and he disposed of many of his wives by banishment or killing them under one pretext or another.

All his male servants were castrated eunuchs, thus assuring that he was the only male in his close quarters.

He had been so angered about not being able to have a child that, after nearly 10 years living as a celibate in anger, he decided to enter into matrimony again.

For his next bride to be, he lined up a dozen young, eligible women from across the land, all daughters of governors or war lords; he asked the best of the clairvoyants, witches, astrologers and magicians to carefully shortlist three candidates from whom he could chose his queen; the one who would provide the male heir.

After much heart searching and discussion, the daughter of an influential governor in the north of the kingdom, who was a national hero for chivalry, was chosen to become the Queen of King Zahhak.

This time the king did not need to wait long before Laleh, the new queen, was announced to be expecting a baby. Celebrations took place throughout the land and some even guessed at the name of the unborn prince.

Nine months later Zahhak's hopes of producing a son were yet again, totally dashed when the newborn was a girl. The baby girl was named Jasmine. She was said to be one of the most beautiful girls anyone had ever seen but every courtier knew that she was doomed.

Zahhak was not only disappointed but was now angry – in fact furious. He ordered the arrest and execution of the astrologer, the clairvoyant, the magician and the witch who had recommended the queen to be the one woman who could have produced a baby boy. In the event, all but the witch were put to death. The executioner was afraid of the consequences of putting a witch to death; therefore, he let her escape but lost his own head.

Zahhak's anger did not even stop at that. He ordered soldiers to search the kingdom and put to death any baby boy born in the same year as Jasmine.

Nevertheless, he had a great problem that he could hardly solve and none of his ministers and friends could, or would, help. He did not quite know what to do with his Queen or his daughter Jasmine because he could not order the execution of Laleh, nor could he just dispose of little Jasmine, because

Laleh's father was an important hero and a governor with a strong army.

What Zahhak decided to do was to banish Laleh to a foreign land. He also ordered the deportation of Jasmine to a cave in Mount Damavand, with its mysteries and legendary inhabitants. This meant that for sure she would die but not directly by his hands.

Mount Damavand and its mysteries

In the northern part of the Persian Empire (Iran of today), along the southern border of the Caspian Sea, there is a chain of mountains called Alborz, of which Mount Damavand, at 5609 metres above sea level, is the highest peak. The Alborz stretches east and west to link with other ranges of mountains in Asia.

Mount Damavand

Damavand has been home for a variety of mythical birds and animals, of which three were notorious and documented in legends and books:

- Simurgh; a very unusual bird
- Azi Dahaka; a monster
- Karkadan; a unicorn.

On the very top of Damavand's peak, hidden by clouds was a tree of life – Gaokerena – in which nested a strange type of creature.

This creature was said to be a huge female bird called *Simurgh*, a peacock with the head of a dog and the claws of a lion. She was agile and powerful, an invincible creature of benevolence, who could catch and lift up into the air large animals and transport them to a long distance with the speed of light. She usually gave her friends and good people a bunch of her feathers, which could be burnt or thrown into the wind to summon her assistance.

This is the oldest image of Simurgh in the Shanameh Ferdawsi indicating the characteristics of the wing, the head and the feet.

Above : An image of Gaokerena (Tree of life)[9]

Below : Simurgh and Gaokerena[10]

9 http://collections.lacma.org/sites/default/files/remote_images/piction/ma-31756956-O3.jpg

10 Gallery:https://commons.wikimedia.org/w/index.php?curid=27308399

In one of the caves, in a rocky chamber on the same mountain was lodged, chained to rocks, the three-headed dragon Aži Dahāka (Azi for short) which was condemned to remain there until the end of the world. This creature was a servant of the devil. Despite being chained, he was able to blow fire when angered and cause the volcano Damavand to erupt and the earth to quake. Nevertheless, his anger could be checked by Simurgh.

Image of Azi Dahaka, a three headed Monster/Dragon

Aži Dahāka is mentioned in the Avesta, the earliest religious texts of Zoroastrianism, the ancient religion of Persia. He is described as a monster with three mouths, six eyes, and three heads, cunning, strong, and demonic.

In another cave of Damavand and within its tunnels, lived another animal, a kind of Unicorn called Karkadann, meaning the Lord of the Deserts. This animal could roam on the green plain below the mountain but would return to its home within the mountain. Karkadann had a thick skin like a rhinoceros but could be as agile as a horse. It had great strength and its skin was stronger than a shield; it could not be penetrated by any arrow or spear. It seems that, apart from the Simurgh, which was the queen of the mountain and the earth, only a maiden of special grace and quality could subdue this mammoth beast.

Images of Karkadann

Jasmine in Damavand

When Zahhak ordered that Jasmine be thrown into the den of the three headed dragon, he was sure that in no time she would be eaten alive by Azi. Although Zahhak knew of the existence of Simurgh, he had no idea of her whereabouts.

So Jasmine was put in the three headed dragon's lodge. Just as Azi had put out one of his three tongues to pull the baby in his mouth, the Simurgh heard her crying. She descended from her nest and cut off the dragon's tongue, with Jasmine resting on it as if it was a soft cradle.

From then on, Simurgh looked after Jasmine as if she were her own chick. She taught her every skill, particularly the art of war and of defending herself with a sword. Additionally, she provided her with a special bow which could fir three arrows at the same time; this, when discharged, could not miss the intended targets.

Zahhak and Freydoon

Freydoon was the son of a noble family related to King Jamshid. He was born in the same year as Jasmine. He was one of the babies who should have been assassinated by the order of Zahhak. When Zahhak's soldiers were ravaging the countryside in search of young sons of the noble families and those of the governors, Freydoon's mother – seeing Zahhak's agents and soldiers coming to her village burning and destroying everything which stood in their way – took her four year old Freydoon and ran to a barn and hid him under pile of hay. She then ran out trying to draw attention from the hidden child. However, she had no chance of escaping from galloping soldiers on horseback who were surrounding her, throwing dozens of lances at her. As if that was not enough, they cruelly beheaded her as she would not tell them the whereabouts of Freydoon.

Freydoon was nearly caught himself, because he ran out of the barn crying and screaming; calling his mother to take him with her. Fortunately, a group of farmers saw the child running from the barn at the tail end of the soldiers who were in pursuit of Freydoon's mother and hid him in a sack of rice they were carrying. They took Freydoon to a nearby forest where he, and many of the men and women from his village stayed in the dense trees, living in harmony with animals and other fugitive families – whilst practicing the art of war.

Freydoon and a small group of men and women were sworn to check the power of Zahhak, whom they thought was the servant of the Devil, along with the three headed dragon. This, however, was no easy task. Zahhak himself was reputed to have two dragons protruding from each arm on demand and under his command.

These dragons were part of the body of Zahhak but needed to be fed separately. To survive, every day each dragon needed the fresh brain of a man. Therefore, two men had to be sacrificed every day for their brains to be used to feed Zahhak's dragons.

Apart from these vicious dragons, Zahhak is said to have been very strong himself. He could break any military shield by a blow from his fist. Besides his bodyguards, he was always flanked by a huge tiger on each side.

In addition to all of these, Zahhak had a favourite beast and ally whom he had locked up in a cave in Mount Damavand, called Azi-Dahaka. This beast was a huge monster dragon with three heads and mouths and many eyes implanted in different parts of its body. Azi-Dahaka possessed feet and hands which were partly tucked in pouches under its skin. The many tongues of this beast were several meters long allowing him to extend them and let animals as big and powerful as a tiger to sit and relax before suddenly being swallowed by the monster.

Freydoon and his little army could only take on a small

division of Zahhak's army in skirmishes in the vicinity of the forest and would always retreat into the wood when the cavalry of Zahhak's forces were chasing them. The forest had a reputation of being haunted and therefore Zahhak's soldiers would not chase Freydoon's men within but always stopped at the edge of trees.

Years passed and Zahhak's reign of terror got worse. He now decided that, as he could not have a son, none of his governors and noble families should have a son, fearing that one of the boys would rebel against him and deprive him of his throne. All of the noble families had to hide their baby boys lest Zahhak would order them to kill their babies or feed them to the three headed dragon.

Despite their huge armies, none of the war lords or heroes would fight Zahhak, whose army's cruelty and savagery in war was notorious. Not only did they fight the soldiers and kill their enemies, but they would burn the villages and torch women and children alive.

When the supply of the brains from the babies of noble families ceased, Zahhak turned his attention to sons of those who worked within the households of the noble families.

Kaveh and Freydoon

Kaveh was a blacksmith working in the stable of one of the governors and thought his little boys were not in danger of being killed because he had no noble blood. Nevertheless, his children were removed from their family homes as their brains were needed to feed the dragons on Zahhak arms. Zahhak ordered the killing of two of Kaveh's sons for their brains to be fed to his personal body dragons. Kaveh wowed to bring down the reign of the tyrant and, in secret, started a revolution.

It is said that after his two children were taken away, Kaveh raised his leather apron on a spear. This became the flag of the revolution known as *Derafsh Kaviani* [image on page 137].

He joined the small army of the eighteen year old boy – Prince Freydoon – who had gathered together to fight the evil Zahhak.

Freydoon's community welcomed Kaveh and his men and, through a series of skirmishes, caused considerable harm to Zahhak's provincial army.

Freydoon and Kaveh, together with a small group of men and women, were sworn to check the power of Zahhak, whom they thought was one of the agents of Ahriman (the Devil) on earth.

Freydoon and his little army could only take on a small division of the Zahhak army and, after months of battles had inflicted heavy losses. In response Zahhak killed a few of his incompetent leaders and decided to take charge of destroying this insignificant rebel. He let it be known that he was set to burn the jungle with its entire population of humans, animals and birds. He wanted a new map of the region to be drawn showing no forest at all in that area of his kingdom of Persia. His plan to burn the trees would flush out men and beasts and he would kill them all. There was nothing or no one to stop him executing such a heinous act.

He assembled his men and knights. He unchained the three headed dragon, Azi-Dahaka, to pull his chariot, in which he stood in full armour flanked by his guards. For the occasion the Devil agreed to activate the two dragons on his shoulders, since these dragons could project fire and poison from their mouths.

He planned to force Freydoon and his army out of the forest by torching the wood and forcing them into a desert called Dasht-e-kavir – a salty, hot desert of some 30,000 square miles in which no one could survive long without appropriate provisions of water and shelter. Freydoon and his men would be in no position to fight; he could torture them and feed them to the lions and other beasts, which were at his command. The head of Freydoon would be hoisted on his standard but the brain reserved as a gala dinner for the dragons on Zahhak shoulders.

So, with due preparation, Zahhak started setting fire to the forest. According to plan, Zahhak's army stood and waited on horseback outside the forest, waiting for Freydoon and his men trying to escape into the desert of the Dasht-e-Kavir.

What Zahhak did not know was that there was a subterranean way (a tunnel) out of the forest leading to the foot of Damavand Mountain which Freydoon and his men used to escape from the burning wood.

Zahhak re-arranged his army quickly. On one side of the battlefield stood many thousands of Zahhak's professional, well equipped army, lined up ready to attack on the signal from their commander. On the other side of the field stood Freydoon riding a white horse, with Kaveh by his side holding the Derafsh Kaviani raised on a spear and riding on a black stallion. They were leading a few hundred men who had limited training. They were ahead of women, children and animals of all kinds who escaped from the inferno. The men and their families were armed with anything they could use to fight; bow and arrow, swords, stones, slingshots, stone throwers, wooden hammers and simple pieces of wood. They were prepared to stand and die with the hope that their death would prompt others to rebel against the evil king.

Freydoon charged with his men towards Zahhak's army. Zahhak waited until he could clearly see Freydoon before lashing Azi to charge towards the white horse. He wanted to personally kill and behead Freydoon whose head would go on his personal banner and whose brain was promised to the two dragons on his arms. Freydoon had the picture of his family, who had been massacred by Zahhak, in his mind and was preparing to join them – but not without a fight. Kaveh could see his little boys snatched by force from his arms until he was beaten unconscious.

As Freydoon, Kaveh and their followers were carrying out their suicidal charge, there was a thunderous noise which reverberated throughout the desert and the mountains. Out of nowhere, a huge unicorn appeared, pulling a stone chariot driven by a beautiful, long haired woman, with armour of diamonds, glowing in the sun and blinding the men in the army of Zahhak.

This was Jasmine, the banished daughter of Zahhak, riding in a chariot of thick stone pulled by the mighty Karkadann, driving to the aid of the white horse of Freydoon and his men. The roaring of Karkadann was enough to frighten the bravest of the men of Zahhak's army. Many ran away and were killed; knight after knight fell – wounded or dead – felled by Jasmine's triple arrows which could not miss their target. All of Zahhak's commanders were killed or ran away.

Zahhak now tried to use the power of the dragons on his shoulders; they too were destroyed by Jasmine's magic arrows.

Zahhak's last refuge was the powerful three headed dragon, Azi-Dahaka, which could turn the desert sand into molten lava and shoot hot ashes into the air from its mouth. It seemed as though the whole field was becoming molten earth.

Now was the time for the supreme help of the Simurgh. Jasmine blew one of the Simurgh feathers into the air. In a moment she arrived and flooded the desert on the side of Zahhak's army; the Azi-Dahaka simply sank and was almost drowned.

The time was now for Freydoon and Jasmine to take on Zahhak and his personal bodyguard. The three bodyguards were easily disposed of by Jasmine; the time for revenge had arrived – Freydoon had witnessed how his mother was chased by Zahhak's men and killed after hiding her him in a barn. Jasmine thought of the cruelty of her father Zahhak who had banished her mother and had nearly succeeded to feed her to Azi in a cave in the mount Damavand. Zahhak was now alone without anyone by his side; he was ready to die at the hands of Freydoon and Jasmin. Sword drawn Freydoon and Jasmin approached the evil king ready to cut him to pieces.

"NO, NO, NO," shouted Simurgh, flying overhead "Do not kill this evil man. Do not wash blood with blood."

At these words the killing was stopped.

The three headed monster Azi-Dahaka and Zahhak were shackled to be transported to one of the caves of Mount Damavand where they were to be chained to the rocks for ever and ever.

Freydoon became the king of Persia and Jasmine his queen.

The cruelty and killing in the kingdom was stopped; law and order were established.

The Simurgh became a symbol of the Persian Kingdom and Empire – the symbol which never left the minds and hearts of any Persian.

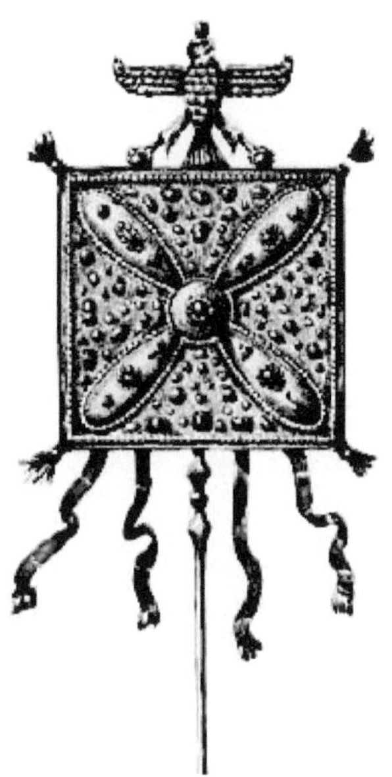

Above: Derafsh Kaviani[11]

Below: The two dragons mounting from Zahhak's arm[12]

11 https://en.wikipedia.org/wiki/Derafsh_Kaviani

12 http://www.zoroastriankids.com/zahhak.html

Dasht-e-Kavir
Layer after layer of sand
for mile after mile

This version of Zahhak is one of the many varieties of the tale. In essence my Zahhak is based on what I was told and read as a child and may not represent the version acknowledged by mythologists. For instance Azi-Dahaka for some mythologists is an alternative name for Zahhak, whereas in my version Azi Dahaka is a monster which serves Zahhak.

As such I have been interested in "story telling" rather than debating the historical mythology.

– Keyvan Moghissi

About the Author

Professor Keyvan Moghissi

BSc, MD, FRCS (Ed), FRCS (Eng), FETCS

Keyvan Moghissi is one of the UK's leading Cardiothoracic Surgeons with many books, papers, articles and presentations to his name.

He was born in Tehran, the Capital City of Iran, into a Baha'i family. He spent his childhood and part of his teens in Tehran, during which time, at 15 years old, he won an important competition in violin, allowing him to study under Abol Hassan Saba – the greatest violinist of Persian Music.

The family then moved to Geneva in Switzerland where they made their home.

He enrolled in the faculty of Medicine of Geneva University where he obtained a first-class degree before embarking on post graduate studies in General and Chest Surgery in Switzerland

and the UK. In parallel with his school and medical studies in 1954 he qualified in violin under Professor Fernand Closset, at the Conservatoire Populaire de Musique de Geneve.

In 1970, he was appointed Consultant Cardiothoracic Surgeon in Hull, with a mission to establish an open heart surgery centre at Castle Hill Hospital.

In the 1970's and 1980's, he became one of the founding fathers of the European Thoracic Surgical Club and the European Association of Cardiothoracic Surgery, for which he served as its second President. He also played a major role in the foundation of the European Respiratory Society (ERS).

In 1985, he undertook pioneering laser surgery of the chest and was the first cardiothoracic surgeon to use laser to remove secondary breast cancer from the lung without loss of lung tissue.

In 1989 he was part of an international team pioneering the use of Photodynamic Therapy (PDT) for lung cancer in the UK and Europe.

Keyvan Moghissi was key to the creation of the Yorkshire Laser Centre – the project of charitable trust, The Moghissi Laser Trust (Registered Charity no 326689).

He has been honoured with membership of L'Academie de Chirurgie (Paris), an honorary Visiting Professorship from *Guang Zhou University* (China) and honorary membership of a number of other international and European Associations. His honours include awards for contribution to science and cardiothoracic surgery from Russia and an award for 'Life long Contribution to Cardiothoracic Surgery' from the World Society of Cardiothoracic Surgery.

His hobbies include languages, classical music and playing the violin.

Last year Keyvan Moghissi's first short story book "Off My Chest" was published on Amazon.

www.ingramcontent.com/pod-product-compliance
Ingram Content Group UK Ltd.
Pitfield, Milton Keynes, MK11 3LW, UK
UKHW041853190726
13854UKWH00002B/870